The Last Sane Man on Earth

Nathan O'Hagan

Published by Armley Press 2020

The Last Sane Man on Earth
Copyright © 2020 Nathan O'Hagan

Published by Armley Press 2020

www.armleypress.com

ISBN: 978-1-9160165-2-1

Layout: Wayne Leeming
Cover design: Eden Read
Copy editing: Wayne Leeming and John Lake
Production: Mick McCann

With thanks to Wayne Leeming, Probe Plus, Steve Rycroft, Russ Litten, Armley Press, Eden Read, James Brown, James Endeacott, my friends and family, and anyone who has been kind enough to read my books.

Grateful acknowledgement is made to Nigel Blackwell for permission to reproduce an excerpt from the following copyrighted material:

'When the Evening Sun Goes Down.'
© 2002 Half Man Half Biscuit

"*The World is (Not) a Dead Cold Place* has everything even immense heart-warming moments. This is not just a story it is about modern life the world in which we all live. You must read this for the moments of pure joy and occasional sadness. But you will come to love this and many will re-visit at a later time. HIGHLY RECOMMENDED."
— The Last Word

"I shout all my obscenities from steeples
But please don't label me a madman."
- *Nigel Blackwell*

Intro

The Prisoner finished his push ups and put his top back on. Behind him, he heard the door to his cell closing and as he turned around he was greeted by the sight of three neo-Nazis.

"Oh, look," he said, stepping back to size them up. "It's the world's most right-wing Bee Gees tribute act. Actually, I'm glad you shit-stains are here. I was about to have a quick wank but you can suck me dick." He said this to the biggest Nazi standing in the middle, then addressed the others. "And you two can suck a bollock each."

"You fucking smart-arsed scouse bastard," the lead Nazi said. "You've been acting the fucking hard man since you got in here. You're gonna get what's coming to you now."

"Alright," The Prisoner said, "tell you what, mate... if you're not into sucking, then you can just sit in the corner and crack one off while you watch me bum-fuck your two little minions. But first, maybe you can explain to me why members of the so-called master race tend to be ugly, thick-as-pig-shit, in-bred, dickless fucking simpletons who all seem to visit the same blind tattooist."

"Fucking left-wing scouse scum," Minion #1 said as the three of them stepped forwards.

Before they'd managed to take a full step, though, The Prisoner had picked up the radio from the tiny table in the corner and was now swinging it around his head by the plug-cord like an ancient meteor hammer. The three men bobbed and weaved on their toes like boxers, waiting for an opening as the radio flew just inches from their faces, making a dull whirring sound in the air. Minion #1 ducked beneath the radio as it made its way on another spin around. As he did so, The Prisoner released it and the radio flew past his head straight into the leader's face. An impressive gash opened between his eyes, a quick stream of blood instantly blinding him. Minion #1 hesitated, the felling of his leader seeming to suddenly sap his valour. The momentary loss of concentration on the task in hand was enough. Before he could even turn back, The Prisoner had taken a step forward, lifted his foot up and brought it directly down onto the top of his knee.

"AAAAAARRRRGH!"

"There!" yelled The Prisoner over the screams. "Try goose-stepping with a cunted up knee, you fucking Nazi maggot!"

Minion #1 went down like a sack of shit, his kneecap taking up temporary residence halfway down his shin. The Prisoner quickly retreated to his mattress, reaching inside through a six-inch slit and pulling out a round, one-foot long piece of wood, smuggled from the woodwork room for an occasion such as this. He swung it down onto the face of Minion #2 – by now frozen to the spot in horror. If the second swing to the side of his head wasn't enough to put him out of the game, hitting his head on the way down certainly was.

The Prisoner knelt down to the lead Nazi, who was still trying to wipe the blood from his eyes. He grabbed the Nazi's head in both hands and leaned in close.

12

"A far-right ideology will ultimately lead only to your destruction or that of your loved ones," he said quietly. "Haven't you ever seen 'American History X'? Oh, and I'm from Birkenhead, you cunt."

He leaned his head back as far as he could and slammed it forward into the Nazi's blood-stained face, knocking him out cold. As he rose to his feet, the last man hobbling attempted to make his escape but collapsed as soon as he tried to put his ruined leg down, opting instead to crawl pathetically towards the door.

"Oi, Romper Stomper! Where the fuck you think you're going?" The Prisoner grabbed the guy's ankles and dragged him back into the cell. "I'm not finished with you yet, pal."

He lifted the man onto his arse, sitting him up in front of the bottom bunk of the bed, and then delivered a good, solid punch to the face to ensure full docility and another one just for fun.

"Right", he said. "I reckon it's a Brown Collar Muffler for you, mate."

He turned around, pulled his trousers down, spread his arse cheeks wide apart, and dropped his crack onto Minion #1's face, whose shriek of disgust was immediately muffled. The aim couldn't have been more perfect. His arse landed with such precision, the Aryan's nose nearly went straight up his anus. The Prisoner released his cheeks, allowing them to clamp onto the side of his casualty's head before unleashing a torrent of farts into his battered face.

"I'm glad I hadn't had the chance to shower after doing me exercises... adds to the flavour for you, doesn't it?"

Beneath him, Minion #1 struggled ineffectually, his smothered screams rippling up through The Prisoner's arse crack.

"Fucking hell, lad!" he shouted. "That actually feels pretty nice. You keep squealing like that, you're gonna give me a fucking hard-on."

Minion #1 finally saw daylight as The Prisoner lifted his arse up. He tried to blink out the methane, gasp in fresh air, but tasted only the brown cloud that had begun to lift from his face. A big pair of dangling balls and a semi-hard cock hovered before him, beneath which the upside-down face of The Prisoner appeared as he bent down and, through his legs, shouted back one word:

"BUCKLE!"

ONE

My walk to work takes me between forty-two and forty-seven minutes, which varies according to factors such as traffic and weather conditions. From my flat, it would take about seventeen minutes by bus but that would mean having to actually get on a bus and probably having to sit or stand next to somebody who may either attack me or, worse yet, start up a conversation with me. So I made the decision just one day into the job to walk the route, regardless of weather conditions, illness or any other factors that might force an ordinary person to reconsider.

Each morning, I leave my flat on Devonshire Road in Aigburth, Liverpool, and walk along Aigburth Road, turn left at the top and turn right onto Park Road, where I make the long walk towards the city centre. It is not a pleasant walk. Though by no means the worst area of Liverpool or Merseyside, it certainly isn't the best, and includes a walk past a Jobcentre Plus (I still haven't ever figured out what the "plus" is), which always induces anxiety to add to the constant backdrop of already-present moderate anxiety. I take the walk at an average pace. If I walked at my optimum speed I could probably shave between seven and ten minutes off the walk but that would mean arriving at work sweaty and needing another shower. There are actually basic shower facilities available at my work place, and by most standards they are kept relatively clean. But I would no sooner use a public shower than I would drink from a public toilet. Unless I knew for certain that the cleaners work to my high standards, there would be too much chance of coming into contact with other people's dead skin cells or standing on a stray pube. This pace is therefore the most sensible option, but I have to quicken my pace slightly when I reach the Jobcentre, even though I am walking on the opposite side of the road at this point.

When I reach the city centre I take as many back streets as possible to reduce exposure to the smog and pollution. The inherent dirtiness of the smaller streets is something that I have, over time, had to balance against the noise and crowdedness of the main streets, and I have concluded that it is the former that is marginally less offensive to me. I reach the corner of Temple Street, where my workplace is located, and, as I do every morning, I stop at Bean Grinder, the coffee shop on the corner. I'm uncertain whether the name of this establishment is a bad attempt at a hilarious, cheeky, pun, or the result of the owner failing to spot the terrible inherent double-entendre. I take a deep breath as I enter, and prepare myself for the onslaught of inanely good-natured and enthusiastic chat from the owner. He's a man in his late twenties with long hair, which he has stuffed back into some sort of hairnet device, and the kind of thick, oiled and groomed beard that seems to now cover the face of just about every fucking man under the age of thirty in the entire country. I don't know his name but have come to think of him as simply The Knobhead.

"Hey, man," he shouts as I enter, whilst rearranging the display of gluten and wheat-free biscuits on the front counter.

"Hello," I say in monotone. I've long since given up trying to pre-emptively counter his friendliness by being rude, non-communicative or aggressive. This man's vigour for life and for serving coffee and food to the people of this city cannot be dented. Every morning I come in and he treats me like an old friend, despite the fact that I have never said more than what is absolutely essential to secure my morning coffee. Either his enthusiasm is genuinely undimmable or he is simply a very astute businessman who strongly believes such manners are the secret to good customer relations. Another possibility, of course, is that he's simply so fucking stupid that he doesn't realise how rude I'm being, and this stupidity allows him to meet the world with such ignorant glee. Personally, I suspect it is a combination of all three, with a heavy emphasis on the third. I hate coming in here but I made the unfortunate discovery a while back that this place does happen to serve some of the best coffee I have ever tasted. Now, the instant coffee I used to bring to work in a flask and the coffee provided at work are unacceptably inferior, and I deeply resent The Knobhead trapping me like this.

"What'll it be today, man?"

"Large black coffee. Takeaway."

"Kewl. Any pastries for ya this morning?"

I haven't yet been able to quite place his accent. It might be a soft Australian or New Zealand accent, possibly a posh southern English one, which has been softened by a mild pot-head drawl. It certainly has an element of scouse twang to it, but that could quite easily have been picked up, or could be as much of an affectation as his laid back demeanour or his annoying fucking hipster beard.

"No. Just the coffee."

"Kewl, kewl. That's three quid please, mate."

I reach into my pocket and take out the small sealable plastic bag containing three one-pound coins and hand it to him. About once every fortnight I do this to use up any change I happen to find knocking about the flat, and every time I do it he looks at the bag and tries to hide his utter fucking befuddlement as he takes it from me and empties the coins into his till.

"You want the bag back?" he says, same as he always does.

"Keep it," I say, same as I always do.

"Er, yeah... kewl, kewl. Okay, you have a good day, man," he says as I walk towards the door, without answering.

As I leave the premises I turn back to see The Knobhead standing at the till, still staring into the bag.

I finally reach my place of work and hold my swipe card to the door. I walk up the stairs to the second floor and through the main outer office, which is mostly deserted. I get just a couple of half-hearted hellos as I pass through. I arrive early enough that there are very few people here yet, and even if the place was full most people know by now not to bother with anything but the most rudimentary of pleasantries with me.

I enter my own small office and close the door. I sit at my desk and take out the mini-hoover I keep in the bottom drawer and I use it to clean the desk, paying particular attention to the computer keyboard. The cleaners will have been in last night, but I have my own specifications. There's no guarantee they won't have left behind their own skin cells, that they won't have sneezed and forgotten or neglected to wipe it up, that they haven't had a shit or a wank immediately before cleaning my desk and not washed their own hands sufficiently. There is absolutely nothing to guarantee that there will be no shit particles or jizz cells deep within the crevices of the keyboard or all over my stationery.

Having hoovered the desk and computer, I spray a layer of my cleaning spray (my own recipe, a mild concoction containing sterile water, lemon juice, white vinegar, baking powder and salt) and wipe it down using wet wipes, which I also keep in the drawer. I return my cleaning products back to the drawer and switch my computer on. I sit back as I watch the email alerts and memos pop up on screen. As I do, I ask myself the same question I ask every weekday morning.

How the fuck did I end up here?

TWO

The company I work for is called CUltureSHock Design. And yes, the capital U, S and H are intentional. I have now been working here for over a year, and I'm still not sure what the company actually does. I know it's a design company, but I'm not sure what it is they design. Something to do with online content, whatever the fuck that is. I think we might be a media branding company. Or a brand media one. Again, I couldn't begin to describe what any of that means. But those are the phrases I most regularly hear, so I'm guessing the output is somewhere in that area. It was described as a "start-up" when I began working here, a term I hear a lot, and one that completely baffles me. Surely all companies are start-ups in that they have all started up at some point?

I came here in utter desperation. My exit from Park Communications left me almost completely unemployable, with no employment history, no references and pretty much no skills. After a few short-term temp jobs as a data entry clerk, the employment agency I had registered with told me about an "exciting new opportunity" in a new "creative start-up" in Liverpool city centre. My first thought was the journey. Did I take the train or the bus? Either way I would be trapped underground with madmen, whether on the Merseyrail network or in the Kingsway Tunnel. After much deliberation, I decided to take the ferry (despite it being more expensive and over twice as long a journey), having concluded that these impediments, as well as having to listen to Gerry Marsden singing "Ferry Cross the Mersey" on repeat, were marginally preferable to having to be stuck underground with the fucking flotsam and jetsam of Birkenhead and the Wirral travelling to Liverpool.

On the trip over for the interview, I sequestered myself in the quietest part of the ferry but experienced a moderate panic attack less than halfway over. Heading up to the top deck to try and compose myself, I briefly considered jumping overboard, and for a moment the prospect of flapping my arms pathetically against the waves before being dragged under, knowing that my bloated, jellyfish-covered corpse would wash up some days later at the feet of an unsuspecting paddler, seemed preferable to having to sit through an interview for a job I didn't want and yet, paradoxically, desperately needed. Naturally, my cowardice ensured I didn't act on my urge. My cowardice, and the fact that I do now have something, one thing, to live for.

When I arrived at CUltureSHock, I instantly realised that, despite not being quite thirty years of age yet, I was the oldest person in the building by a good few years. I was also completely overdressed, being the only person wearing a shirt and tie. I was shown into a meeting room by a young man wearing knee-length denim shorts, sandals and a pair of glasses which were clearly designed to give the retro NHS specs look, and which I strongly suspected contained plain glass. He looked at my shirt and tie combination like he had never seen one before, and sat me in the office.

"Eddie will be through in a minute," he said.

"Who's Eddie?"

"He's the boss. But he doesn't really like words like boss, that's a bit too conservative for him."

"Right. So, what is he then?"

The lad thought for a moment. "Erm, well I suppose he's the boss."

"Right. Thanks for that."

I looked at the room, with framed pictures of Jobs, Zuckerberg and a quote attributed to the former painted on the wall. I waited for about ten minutes, during which I considered sneaking out, hiding in a cupboard or jumping through the window. Just as I was about to take the first option, Eddie walked in. Well, when I say "walked", a more accurate description would be to say he skipped in with all the enthusiasm of a child being let into a sweet shop.

"Hi, Gary, right? I'm Eddie," he said, stretching out his hand. I reluctantly stretched out my own only to see that he wasn't offering a handshake but a fist bump. My initial disgust at being offered a fist bump by another white man was quickly tempered by the knowledge that, by replacing a handshake with this particular form of greeting, Eddie was actually reducing the amount of germs likely to pass between us. The germs and dead skin cells that did pass onto me would be localised to the back of my hand, significantly reducing the likelihood of said germs and cells then being passed onto a more important part of me, such as my mouth or face, which they might have done had they been passed onto my palm. My relief at this did little to offset the instant contempt I felt for the man, if I could call him that; my first estimate placed him at about twenty-three years of age, making him probably the second eldest person in the building after myself. He sat down on the couch beside me.

"Can I get you a coffee?"

"No, I'm fine."

"Okay, cool. Down to business then. Let me tell you a bit about CUltureSHock. I started the place up about eighteen months back, renting a little office the other side of town, just me running the place and two other guys working for me. Since then we've expanded as the company's grown and we set up here about six months ago. What we're looking for right now is someone to join our crew to help collate our output and to deal with some incoming enquiries. You're computer literate, yeah?"

"Well, yes, but..."

"All our software is designed in-house, so we'll need to train you up on that, but it's real simple, mega-user-friendly, yeah?"

Confused as to whether the "yeah?" was actually a statement or an unclear question, I simply nodded along.

"As you've probably already noticed, the vibe here is chilled but also real energetic at the same time?"

Again, the upwards inflection at the end of the sentence left me unclear whether I was being asked a question or a statement was being made. Again, I nodded along. At this point, Eddie completely lost me with talk of "content" and "branding". I continued my nodding dog impression, trying to understand at least some of what was being said.

"So, any questions so far?"

"Erm... yeah, I was under the impression this was a data-entry type position?"

"Well, to be honest with you, Gary, we don't really like terms like that. Yeah, there's an element of data entry and collating, but we find that terms like that stifle people's creativity. We prefer to just let people find their own niche here. You know, let *them* figure out what it is they can bring to the table, rather than being all, like, 'yeah, this is your box here, you fit inside that box'. I guess we kind of want you to construct *your own* box and see what you can throw out of it, yeah?"

He seemed to now be struggling with his own box analogy, so cut himself short.

"Okay, so when can you start, Gary?"

"Start?"

"Yeah, when can you start?"

"Oh. I thought... don't you have other people to see?"

"Well we do, but I'm gonna be honest with you here, Gary. I'm getting a pretty good vibe from you right now, and I like to go with my instincts on most things, recruitment included."

Quite where he was detecting this "vibe" was beyond me. The only vibe I could possibly have been giving off was one of quiet desperation. I wondered whether he'd maybe done a mid-morning line of coke before meeting me, and his gacked-up mind was mistaking my nervousness for some modicum of brooding charisma.

"Also, Gary, I think – frankly – we could do with an older head round here. You know... bring a different perspective to things."

"Old? I'm not even fucking thirty!" I blurted out without thinking. I expected to be asked to leave immediately, which I felt would probably have been the best solution for all involved. To my surprise, Eddie let out a burst of laughter.

"Yeah, yeah, like it man, like it. That's what I'm talking about... you've got a bit of an edge to ya. The rest of these guys here, they're all super-creative, but most of them are straight from uni, ya know? I really think having someone here who's been around the block a bit is just what we need."

I decided not to point out that the only block I had been around was the one at the end of my street.

"So, how would you feel about starting on Monday then, Gary?"

*

That interview was nearly twelve months ago. For the first few months, I simply went in every morning, kept my head down and tried to look like I knew what I was doing. The money wasn't great, but it was significantly more than I earned during my brief time at Park. I worked from half eight till half four, Monday to Friday, with the occasional half day on a Saturday.

After a few months, my job "evolved" into essentially tracking what was "trending" across social media and writing short reports for Eddie on my findings. This is, of course, mind-numbingly boring, but, on the plus side, I was instantly all but shunned by my co-workers. That age difference Eddie had alluded to seemed to be a significant factor in this, along with the fact that I set my stall out from the start, only ever giving terse responses to attempts at conversation. As I have found out more than once, giving in to the social conventions of small-talk, or even anything beyond basic civility, gives out the wrong signals. This, combined with the fact that I often wore earplugs at work to block out the sound of whatever trendy, pseudo-electronic musical shite was filling the office, meant I was mostly just left alone. The people there, at best, tolerated me or, in most cases, displayed as much contempt towards me as I felt towards them.

All, that is, except for Eddie. Whatever impression I had unwittingly made in our first meeting had lasted. He greeted me with enthusiasm each time he saw me, often praising me in front of other staff and tolerating my moodiness and occasional outbursts when my self-control was lacking. One morning, I had to go into his office while he was talking to another member of staff. When he asked if I had finished the latest report, I snapped back that it'd be ready when it was ready.

"Yeah, cool, no worries," was the response I received, when a paperweight being thrown at my head might have been what I deserved. As I left the office I overheard him speaking to my co-worker.

"See, that's what I'm talking about. Proper maverick sensibility, yeah?"

So, in some way that I couldn't quite understand, I had become a valued member of the team, indulged by my boss, whose liking for me seemed to increase regardless of what I said or did. But the best was yet to come.

Six months into my tenure, CUltureSHock was bought out by another, much larger company. Initially, the news of this filled me with dread, the prospect of a big company coming in and putting more structure in place was

26

terrifying, but I needn't have worried. Eddie struck a deal with the firm – who I probably should have heard of, but hadn't – whereby he maintained complete control over the day-to-day running of the company. Best of all, the incoming investment allowed him to create three new positions, one of which went to me. So in the blink of an eye, I went from a temp to a permanent member of staff – a "Social Media Analyst" – with a salary of £22k per annum. This may not sound like huge money to most people, but to me it was a fortune, and didn't include several performance related bonuses on offer.

Frankly, I didn't have the slightest inclination to strive for the bonuses; the basic pay was more than enough for me. The best part of the new arrangement, however, was that I was given an office, away from the main room where most people worked. It may have been a tiny office, with barely enough room to fit a desk in, but it was perfect for me; it had a toilet nearby which was out of the way of most of the office, so once I got to work, it wasn't uncommon for me to go the entire day without having to interact with a single other person. There were emails, some phone calls, and I would have to grit my teeth through hour-long monthly meetings, but even these were made gradually more bearable by virtue of the fact that, after the first few, people tended not to ask me for my input, given my propensity for swearing. This "maverick sensibility" image was a real asset. Other than these minor intrusions, I was, for the most part, left alone. It got to a point I never thought I could reach in a workplace. I was, relatively speaking, comfortable.

THREE

The walk home is, strangely, worse than the one into work. Despite the growing feeling of impending doom that the walk in brings, the sense of dread helps to block out the surrounding shit of the streets. But during the walk home, after eight hours of staring at a computer screen, I find that I just want to get back and shut the door on the outside world.

I reach the flat and slam the door shut. I slide the bolt across and turn the mortis lock. I close the bolt at the top of the door, followed by the one at the bottom. I then unlock them all in reverse order, before locking them again. I put my coat on the hook next to the door and place my bag on the floor directly underneath it. I walk through to the kitchen, where Jenny is preparing dinner, as she always gets home about twenty minutes before me. She turns around to greet me and I kiss her seven times.

"Back soon," I say to her, and go through to the bedroom.

I close the door and take my clothes off. I don't wear a suit to work. To do so, of course, would be frowned upon at CUltureSHock. Eddie encourages his staff to wear whatever they feel comfortable in. In the case of my co-workers, this seems to mean tight white T-shirts with a bizarre plunge-necked cleavage, three-quarter-length shorts, and what I can only describe as ballet shoes. And this is in the winter. Eddie no doubt believes this is creating an atmosphere of freedom and creativity. And for most of them it probably is, but not for me.

As much as I hate wearing a suit, I appreciate the lack of thought and planning that comes with being forced to wear them; you buy or two or three inexpensive suits, a shirt for each day with one spare in case of emergencies, two ties (in case one gets soiled, ripped or stolen) and a pair of simple black shoes. In some situations, uniformity and conformity are good things. Eddie, in his attempts to create a workplace without rules, gave me one of the most stressful weekends of my life as I had to navigate the shopping centre of Liverpool in a quest to find suitable work clothing.

What was a twenty nine-year-old, hopelessly out of place and out of his depth, supposed to wear to a "creative/casual" office? Sorry, not office. The "O" word is banned at CUltureSHock. Instead, we are instructed to use the word "hub". But my usual uniform of jeans and T-shirts were not going to pass muster, and a suit wasn't an option. My mum insisted on taking me to buy some new work clobber at her expense. Going on a clothes buying trip for work clothes with my mum was as enticing a proposition as going to buy school uniforms used to be, but I acquiesced, mainly because it meant I wouldn't have to spend money on clothes I didn't want, and resented having to buy. After two hours of shopping, during which I had three full-blown panic attacks, I settled on three pairs of dark jeans, slightly smarter than the ones I would normally wear, a selection of smart/casual grey shirts which were slightly smarter than the T-shirts I usually wear, and two pairs of dark trainers, slightly smarter than my usual ones, which at a glance probably looked more like shoes.

I take my jeans off and hang them in the wardrobe. It's only Monday, so they will be good for at least one more day. I take off my shirt and carefully fold it, before placing it into my laundry bin, which is situated on my side of the room. I take off my socks and underwear and place them into the smaller laundry bin. I place a large towel on the centre of the bed, and lie back on it, naked. I close my eyes, and stretch out in a star shape. I breathe slowly in for seven seconds, before breathing out for eleven. I repeat this for as long as I feel necessary on any given evening, but it usually lasts about five minutes. I then curl up into a ball, tensing every single muscle in my body, balling my hands into tight fists, even my toes curled in as far as possible, breathing in as deep as I can, before then unfurling every limb and relaxing every muscle, while simultaneously blowing out the breath as hard as I can. This process is also repeated as many times as necessary, again, usually lasting about five minutes.

This is what I call my nightly "decompress". I do this, without fail, every time I get home from work. When I'm finished, I pick up the towel and go to the bathroom. I switch on the shower and stand under the hot water for exactly ten minutes, scrubbing myself with a thick loofah, which I have just taken out of the packet. I pay particular attention to the shirt line around my neck, trying to get as much of the grime as possible out. I take a small nail brush out of its packet and scrub hard upon – and between – my toes. Two long walks each day means particular attention is needed here. When I'm finished I step out of the shower and wrap the nail brush and loafer back up in their packaging and place them both in a plastic bag which I tie shut and put into the bathroom bin.

I walk back to the bedroom and put on a pair of thin tracksuit bottoms and a T-shirt. Approximately twenty-five minutes after returning home, I'm now ready, sufficiently cleansed of my day in the office to sit with Jenny and eat dinner. After my first night at work, it was clear I couldn't sit with Jenny without going through this routine. The decompress was needed to rid myself of the tension that had built up through the day, and the shower is necessary because I felt like, without it, I was physically bringing work into the flat, somehow sullying what we had here.

I sit at the table, upon which Jenny has already set and placed dinner. I'm comfortable with this seemingly chauvinistic set-up as it only occurs Monday through to Thursday. I do all the weekend cooking, and am responsible for the cleaning of the flat in its entirety. Within a few days of us moving in together, it was clear Jenny's standards of cleanliness, whilst by no means low, were always going to fall far short of mine, so I insisted the cleaning be solely my remit, an arrangement Jenny was more than happy to agree to. The only stipulation she made was that I leave her side of the bedroom for her to clean. I'm not entirely comfortable with this aspect of our arrangement, as Jenny can often leave her side of the room in a state of moderate disrepair for two or three days at a time. My hope is that over time she will either improve her standards or allow me to contribute or supervise. Hopefully over not very much time.

"Good day?" Jenny asks, pouring us a glass of wine each. I take a bite of my lasagne and chew it slowly as I consider the question.

"Define 'good'."

"Erm... was it a glorious, fulfilling endeavour that made you feel lucky to be a part of... whatever unspecified creative activities take place at your workplace?"

"Then no. It wasn't good."

"Okay, was it a crushing, soul-destroying grind that made you want to hang yourself from the ceiling?"

I snap off a piece of garlic ciabatta, and take a big swig of wine. "No."

"Well, maybe we can classify it as a good day then."

"I'd probably rather shoot myself than hang myself. Having first taken a massive overdose. Less chance of it going wrong."

"But if you took a massive overdose first, then you might lose consciousness before you're able to shoot yourself, and the overdose might not work, leaving you with, say, liver damage. Or the overdose might just make you drowsy, and you might end up fucking up the shooting. Maybe you'd blow your jaw off but not kill yourself, then you'd have to live without a jaw, or undergo extensive surgery to rectify it."

I'm already shaking my head before she's even finished her point.

"No, no. All you need to do is have the gun loaded and ready to go, *then* take the overdose. As soon as you've taken it, like the very instant it's been ingested, or injected or whatever, then all you've gotta do is pull the trigger. In all likelihood, each act in itself will have been sufficient to kill you, it's just making doubly sure by combining the two. If you wanted to truly 'triple-lock' the entire endeavour, then you could always take the overdose while standing by a river or canal, with rocks in your pockets. Then you could shoot yourself as you lean backwards over the water. Your natural momentum as you shoot yourself would very probably send you into the water where, failing all else, you'd almost certainly drown. Leaving very little if anything to chance."

Jenny takes a sip of her own wine, nodding subtly as I make my points. "Okay, noted. So, did your day make you feel as though you wanted to take a large overdose, and immediately put a gun in your mouth near open water?"

"No," I say after a pause, "I don't recall feeling those particular impulses today."

"Alright then, I suppose we can say, as it didn't lead you to seriously consider ending your life, we can indeed classify this as a good day. Or satisfactory at least."

"I wouldn't go that far. I don't think I could honestly say anything I did today brought me the slightest bit of satisfaction."

"Perfunctory then?"

I nod slowly as I search my brain for the definition of the word.

"Perfunctory. Yeah," I say.

"Alright then, you had a perfunctory day."

"I did. I had a perfunctory day."

I lower my head and carry on eating my lasagne, adding some black pepper to it. I can feel eyes burning a hole through my skull into my brain. I look up and Jenny is staring at me.

"What?" I say.

She says nothing

"Oh, erm. It's not bland or anything, I just wanted some more pepper, that's all. You know I like pepper."

Her expression grows sterner as I speak, and I sense it isn't the use of condiments that has infuriated her.

"What?" I say again. "Oh, right. Sorry. And how was your day?"

She downs the rest of her wine. "Satisfactory," Jenny says. She stands up, takes her plate over to the sink and leaves the kitchen.

I add some more pepper to my lasagne.

FOUR

"And do you feel that Jenny was entitled to feel upset?"

"Fucking hell, I dunno. Maybe."

Kate writes something down in her notepad, whilst somehow managing to maintain eye contact with me. "Maybe?"

"Alright," I say. "She was entitled. Perfectly entitled. It's yet another example of my utter ineptitude with relationships."

"Ineptitude?"

This is a trick that Kate employs frequently. A single-word question in response to something I've said, and somehow it makes me spill my guts.

"Yes, ineptitude. I just don't know what I'm doing. I don't understand how it all works. I've had fuck all practice at this."

"At what?"

"At being... interested in other people. For years I've gone out of my way to avoid talking to other people about their shit. Because I simply wasn't interested. I never tried to fake an interest, never mind actually cultivate one. Now I'm in a situation where I'm *obliged* to take an interest in someone else's affairs. *Every day.* And I don't know how to do it. I don't even know how to fake it."

"Should it be necessary to fake it? Are you not genuinely interested in Jenny's day?"

"Honestly? I don't think I am."

"Really? This is a person with whom you've chosen to take what was, to you, a massive step. Moving in with someone is a massive step for most people, but for you, we know that it required more effort than most. And yet you say you're not interested in her?"

"No," I correct her. "I didn't say I'm not interested in *her*. Don't put words in my fucking mouth."

Kate holds up her hand to stop me. "Gary, that's not acceptable."

"What?"

"You know what, Gary. Swearing in here is fine, if that's how to choose to express yourself, but swearing *at* me is not acceptable. We established these ground rules some time ago, and you agreed to them. If you swear at me again, this session will be brought to a premature close."

I hold my hands up. "I'm sorry."

"Apologies aren't necessary, let's just try not to repeat the behaviour, please."

Therapy with Kate is very different to therapy with Brian. I could have sat and sworn at Brian for a solid hour and he would have just nodded along and taken notes. In fact, that actually happened on many occasions. Most sessions, come to think of it. Kate, on the other hand, doesn't indulge my shit. She'd think nothing of cutting a session short should she consider my behaviour in any way threatening or inappropriate, and has done so before now. This is just one of many ways in which she is better than Brian. But, of course, I'd probably get better psychotherapy from a dominatrix on a phone sex line than I ever got from Brian.

"Okay, it's not that I'm not interested in Jenny. I *am* interested. I'm just not interested in the minutiae of every single aspect of her day. I don't really care about the ins and outs of her job. It's not something I care about. I understand that it's important to have a source of income. And I'm glad that she's successful in her job, I really am. *That's* important to me. In fact, if she could just come home and say 'my job continues to be fulfilling, and I continue to conduct myself well in it', I'd be able to say 'good, I'm glad' and then we could move on. But it's the having to feign interest in all the tiny details that does my head in. The details about meetings and intra-office politics and things like that. I just don't care."

"Playing devil's advocate, is there something else at play here, Gary?"

"Like what?"

"Well, is it possible that, on some level, you find it hard to show interest because, subconsciously, you are resentful?"

"Resentful of what?"

"Jenny's success. I know you have your own job, and I know it pays reasonably well. But you've made it clear you find the job in no way fulfilling, whereas Jenny does actively enjoy her work. And she earns considerably more money than you. I know your wage is reasonable, but many men feel threatened or emasculated by their partners earning more than them."

"Oh, I couldn't care less about that. Honestly, I'd be more than happy if she earned so much that I never had to work at all. So, if I can just play devil's twatvocate, let's be very clear that I really couldn't give any less of a fuck about that."

"Alright, but shouldn't it still be easier for you to take an interest in Jenny's day-to-day happenings? Isn't somebody's work part of who they are?"

"I don't agree with that. I know many people do, but it's just not something that matters to me. A person is more than just their job. And Jenny, of all people, is more than her job. It's perhaps the least important part of who she is, and not caring about her job doesn't mean I don't care about her, it just means I focus on what's genuinely important, and her work is not a part of that."

Kate nods. "It's an interesting distinction," she says, not entirely convincingly. "Alright, let's leave that particular topic there for this week. We can revisit this at a later date. We've still got ten minutes or so left. I was wondering if you'd like to talk about other aspects of your relationship."

"Like what?" I say nervously.

"Well, specifically, I was wondering how things were in your sex life. Has there been any improvement in that—"

"I'm sorry," I cut her off. "I'm really not ready to talk about that again right now."

"Is there any particular reason for—"

"LOOK!" I take a breath and lower my voice. "Look, I'm just not gonna talk about that. Not now, at least. Maybe not at all."

"Okay." She accepts defeat this time. "We'll leave things there for today then, Gary. I'll see you next week."

I sit in my chair for a moment.

"Unless there's anything else you'd like to discuss?"

"No," I say after a few seconds. "Nothing. See you next week."

FIVE

A dark screen. We are looking through the lens of a camera as it moves slowly through what looks like a carpark. A carpark behind a supermarket. The screen shakes slightly as the camera operator stumbles. Lurid pink text appears on the screen: "Glory Hole Pranks". In the bottom left corner, smaller text tells us our location: "Behind the Co-op. Lampings Lane, Bedfordshire".

The text fades as we approach two large dumpsters, between which there is a large, wall-sized sheet of plaster. As we reach the wall we see a hole is cut into it. The image cuts out, before returning a few seconds later, still focussed on the hole in the wall. We hear a low, muffled male voice on the other side of it, before an erect penis appears through it.

On our side of the wall, a young woman appears, with a mask over her eyes. She takes the penis in her hands and begins to masturbate it. She then puts it in her mouth and sucks it. We can hear the moans of pleasure coming from the other side of the wall. The woman takes the penis out of her mouth and continues to masturbate it. As she does so a hand reaches round from behind the camera, wearing a rubber washing up glove. The hand takes hold of the penis just as the woman releases it from her gentle grip.

Again, the camera shakes as it is seemingly passed from one person to another. When it refocuses the woman has gone, and all we can see is the penis held in the gloved hand. The man on the other side seems oblivious as he continues to moan. The gloved hand makes a few gentle, masturbatory strokes before lifting it up towards the belly, to its maximum point, before then yanking it down as far as it will go. The moans are instantly replaced by a loud scream, before the penis disappears from view through the hole. The camera operator runs around to the other side of the hole, where a fat middle-aged man is lying on the floor, his trousers around his ankles. His hands are cupped around his genitals, and blood can be seen seeping through them. The camera zooms in on his face, contorted in pain and confusion.

"You alright there, mate?" a male voice shouts. "Tell you what, we'll call you an ambulance, shall we?"

The screen goes blank as we hear an audio clip being played over it.

"Hello, what is the nature of your emergency?"

"Yeah, er, some fella's ripped his cock here, love."

"I beg your pardon?"

"I said some fella's ripped his cock."

"He ripped his what?"

"His cock, love. You know, his penis, like. It's ripped."

"Where are you calling from, sir?"

"Round the back of the Coey on Lampings Lane. I'm not sure what happened to him. I suppose maybe a fox bit his cock or something, but it looks ripped to me. I'd get an ambulance here for him, if I was you."

Dial tone. Blank screen.

SIX

Dad looks over at me, hesitating.

"Go on, Paul," Kate urges.

This is our first attempt at family therapy. Personally, I don't see the point. I'm more than comfortable with my lack of relations with the rest of them, but it's something Kate has been urging me to try for some weeks now. I'd ignored her for a while, but a few weeks back Jenny mentioned that she'd been thinking it was a good idea. She told me it'd make her happier in the long term if I attempted to build some bridges with my family. Well, my parents, at least. She met Ben briefly, once, and she thought he was a twat too. I agreed to give family therapy a try purely for Jenny's benefit, but Mum and Dad insisted Ben be part of the equation. Ben has, for some reason, agreed to take time out of trying to salvage the fortunes of his latest company to be here. Having sold all remaining shares in the chain of mobile phone shops that made him rich, Ben had set up a new company – Clin-Ex – which provided surgical swabs and other medical equipment to hospitals and surgeries, and the company was now struggling, something my brother laughably blamed on NHS inefficiency, and used as an argument in favour of it being privatised.

"Well, I just can't help but feel we've failed. Jan and me, I think we've failed. As parents."

"How so?"

Dad looks over at me again, and then at Ben. "Well, it's hard to put into words –"

I interrupt him. "Because I'm a cunt, and so is he?" I point over at Ben, who glares at me, but doesn't say anything.

"Gary, that's not constructive," Kate says.

"Of course it is. He's struggling to articulate just how he feels he's failed as a parent, and I'm helping him out. They," I say, pointing at Mum and Dad, "have produced two children; me and him. I don't need to explain to you just how much of a fuck-up I am, and if you haven't already surmised it for yourself, Kate, I can assure you that my brother is a very different kind of fuck-up. A man so utterly devoid of any substance that he has to buy a house big enough to accommodate a rugby team for his wife and only child to live in."

"Oh, here we go," Ben says, suddenly finding his voice. "This is what it comes down to between me and you, Gary. You're jealous of my success, always have been. You've done nothing with your life. Nothing. And you just can't handle seeing me achieve what I've – what are you laughing at?"

"The fact that you still think I could possibly give any less of a fuck about how much money you've got in your bank account, and the fact that you still seem to think being rich is gonna add some inches to your dick, or at least make you remarkable in some way. Let me tell you, Ben, so you can finally stop deluding yourself. You. Will never. Be.

Remarkable. Alright? No matter how much money you have. Although, no doubt that'll be considerably less when the divorce comes through, eh?"

"Gary!" Now it's Mum's turn to pipe up. "That's a horrible thing to say. Families are meant to support each other at difficult times, not mock each other. Besides, your brother's not getting divorced."

"Oh no? So why is he pottering around that fucking ego mansion of his on his own like Citizen fucking Kane? Have his wife and child just gone on an extended holiday at his mother-in-law's?"

"You fucking little—"

"Okay, everyone, let's just take a moment." Kate cuts him off before he can lunge out of his chair at me. "Let's all just take a breath and calm down."

Ben continues to glare at me while we all do the breathing exercise Kate has taught us. I decide to stop the breathing exercise, and relax myself another way; by deliberately antagonising my brother. I wink at him, and he narrows his eyes at me. I silently mouth the word "cunt" at him, and he stands up.

"Right, that's it... I've had enough of this shit!"

"Ben," my mum shouts. "Sit down, will you? We're meant to be trying to make this work, you can't just storm out like this."

"I'm not spending another moment in the same room as *that* prick," he says, pointing his finger close to my face. I hold my hands up in mock innocence.

"I don't think that kind of language is very conducive to family therapy, Benjamin," I say.

"Oh fuck off, Gary. You're such a... a... fucking..."

"What am I, Ben? It's okay, this is a safe space. You can express yourself freely. There's no judgement here."

"Ben, just sit down, will you?" my Dad says.

"You... you fucking..."

I can see tears beginning to well in his eyes. Kate stands up slowly.

"Perhaps you should take a seat."

"Kate," I say, "I'm feeling a little threatened here. Ben's body language is very aggressive and intimidating, and it feels like I'm about to be attacked by an overweight Dominic fucking Raab."

"Gary, please..."

I look up at Ben, and can see his fist clenching. Out of view of everyone, I wink at him again. His face contorts with rage and he takes a swing at me. I see it coming, though, and simply move my head to the side. From his standing position, he has to bend slightly to throw his lame punch, putting him instantly off balance. His fist hits the wood on the back of my chair and he falls on top of me. I use his momentum to shove him off me and onto the floor, where he lands with a dull Tory thud. Several shouts of "Ben!" only partially cover the sound of him yelping. He gets up and walks towards the door.

"Fuck this!" he shouts back as he leaves. "Fuck the lot of you!"

"See you later, Brexit Bollocks," I call out.

He comes back into the room. "I'll have you know, I voted Remain," he shouts.

"Yeah, of course you fucking did, Boris. Like I actually give a shit which fucking way you voted anyway, soft shite."

He looks as though he's about to take another swing at me, but turns and leaves.

"Say hello to the wife and kid for me," I shout as the door slams.

"Well," I say, turning back to everyone else. "I thought that went very well."

SEVEN

"Sounds like it was a resounding success then."

I'm sitting with Jenny in a bar/restaurant on Lark Lane, and I've just told her how the family therapy session unfolded.

"I'd say so, given how low my expectations were anyway."

"And he just took a swing at you? For no fucking reason?"

"Yep. Couldn't believe it."

I cut another piece of steak off and dip it in the mustard.

"And you did nothing to antagonise him?"

I shake my head, without looking up.

"Nothing?"

"You met the guy, he's a prick."

"Yeah, he is, but he didn't seem the type to go round throwing punches at people, Gary. He looked more like the type who'd shit himself and hand over his wallet, Smartphone and car keys if a black person asked him for directions."

I pretend I haven't heard her and look amongst the condiments for some mayonnaise. "No fucking mayo?" I say.

"Never mind the fucking mayo."

47

I put my hand up to attract a waiter's attention and he comes over. "Could I have some mayonnaise, please?"

"I'm sorry, we don't have any mayonnaise."

"You've run out of mayonnaise?"

"No, we haven't run out, we just don't have it."

"What do you mean, you don't have it?"

"Gary, it doesn't matter," Jenny says, but I keep looking at the waiter.

"We just don't have it," he says. "We don't use it."

"Well, *you* might not use it, but I wanted to dip me chips in some mayo. I'm sure lots of people do."

"Nobody's ever asked for it before."

"What, nobody has ever asked for mayonnaise? Ever? Not once?"

The waiter shrugs his shoulders.

"Just leave it, Gary."

"Are you lying to me?" I say to the waiter.

"No. We just... we don't have it."

I rub my eyes. "Right, here on the condiments rack you brought me, I can see, at a glance, five different types of mustard, some horseradish, some tartar sauce, some smoky barbeque sauce, two different types of chilli sauce, mint jelly, redcurrant jelly and cranberry sauce. You have all these, but you're telling me that, nowhere in this building, in the fridge or the cupboard, or anywhere else, do you have one single bottle or jar of mayonnaise? Not even a single sachet?"

"For fuck's sake," Jenny says, dropping her cutlery and sitting back in her chair.

The waiter shrugs again. "I could get you some olive tapenade."

"*Olive tapenade?*"

"Yeah, it's olives, blended together with capers and—"

"Yeah, I know what olive tapenade is. I just don't see it as a suitable alternative to mayonnaise."

"Look," Jenny says to the waiter, "maybe you can just suggest to your manager or the chef or whatever that maybe you could start stocking mayonnaise. And *you*," she says, turning to me, "learn to eat your chips without fucking mayonnaise."

She stands up, picks up her coat from the back of her chair and walks out, leaving her dinner unfinished.

"Shall I get the tapenade, then?" the waiter says as Jenny leaves.

"No, best just get me the bill, please."

He hurries away and I quickly finish my steak, cramming as many chips as possible into my mouth. I pay the bill and catch up to Jenny just as she gets to the flat.

"What's up?" I say around the last mouthful of steak and chips.

"What do you *mean*, what's up?" She slams the door behind us. "What's up is you acting the fucking prick in a restaurant."

"I wasn't acting the prick, I just wanted some mayonnaise."

"Oh, fuck off, Gary. It was fuck all to do with the mayonnaise. It was to do with your family therapy session."

"Was it fuck."

"Of course it was. As soon as I started asking you about what actually happened, you gave me some bullshit about your brother trying to murder you, then decided to be rude to a fucking waiter to deflect the issue."

"I wasn't rude, I was incredulous."

"You were fucking rude to him, Gary," she says. "It's not his fault the restaurant doesn't have mayonnaise."

"I never suggested it was his fault... not directly his fault, anyway." I start putting all the locks on the door. "But, at that moment, he was the face, the embodiment of the system that had taken that ridiculous decision, and therefore became the focus of my frustration. It wasn't personal."

Jenny walks through to the kitchen and gets herself a glass of water.

"Gary, I asked you to attempt these family therapy sessions partly for me, because I want to have the chance to get to know your family, because I believe it's important if we're going to have a future together, and it'll be difficult for me to do that if you don't have a relationship with them. Your brother seems like a total cock, and I don't really care if your relationship with him is beyond repair. But if you treat these sessions as an excuse to wind him up to the point where he physically fucking attacks you, then that means you're not taking them seriously, and you're not taking my wishes seriously. Now, if you try to tell me one more time that you didn't provoke him, then I'm not gonna be able to trust anything else you say. You and I both know the truth, so don't fucking insult my intelligence by pretending otherwise. Okay?"

I nod my head. "Alright, I wound the fucker up. I can't help it. I felt entirely justified. Still do, if I'm being honest."

"Well, at least you're being honest. Just promise me you'll make more of an effort with your parents in these sessions, okay? And Ben, if he comes back."

"Yeah, alright. I'll try. I'm sorry. My Ben-trolling was entirely to fuck with him, not to go against your wishes."

She takes a sip of her water and puts the glass down, and steps towards me. "Fair enough," she says, and hugs me. I hug her back, and her hands move down to my arse and give it a squeeze.

"Right," I say, quickly but gently breaking away from her. "I'd best get a shower before bed."

EIGHT

"Fucking fuck off!"

I punch my computer monitor and look away from it. My eyes are strained and my head aches from spending the last few hours staring endlessly at Twitter, Instagram, Facebook and Pinterest on my PC and the tablet I'm provided with, tracking trends in certain locations around the world, trying to piggyback onto the most popular current hashtags and searches, linking it all into hashtags of my own from the official CUltureSHock social media accounts, with which I have inexplicably been entrusted. Before coming here, I'd never been on Facebook or Twitter, and I'd never even heard of Instagram or Pinterest. Now, via the series of bizarre flukes and misunderstandings that have ensured my continuing employment here, and the stupidity and lack of character assessment possessed by my boss, I am suddenly responsible for all social media output of a pretty successful design firm. I'm still not entirely sure what it is we design. In fact, I'm not even sure "design" is the right term, but it's now far too late to ask anyone, and extensive Google searches and scourings of my own company's website have so far proved inconclusive. There's lots of info on the website, but none of it makes the slightest bit of sense to me.

Regardless, the constant staring at computer screens is causing me eye strain and headaches on a daily basis, which are no doubt exacerbated by the frustration that comes with not knowing what the fuck I'm doing. I put my head on the desk and close my eyes, breathing deeply. I hear the door to my office open, and quickly sit up, trying to disguise my head-on-desk position by pretending to have been looking for something. Standing in the doorway is a lad who calls himself "Dylan", even though I'm pretty sure his name is actually Kevin. He's wearing a Jim Morrison T-shirt, his curly, unkempt hair somewhere between that of Morrison and Harry Potter.

"Er, hi, Gary," he says, entering the office hesitantly.

"Hello, Kev – I mean Dylan."

"Hi," he says again, looking around my office. A short silence ensues while I wait for him to tell me what he wants.

"Is there something you need?" I say when I quickly tire of the pregnant pause.

"No... no I'm fine thanks, man."

Another silence follows.

"Kev – Dylan, I wasn't offering you refreshments. I mean, is there a reason why you're here? Do you need to ask me something?"

"Oh, right, yeah, sound, nice one," he says in a half-stoned drawl. I'm sure most of these young fools are stoned half the time. I marvel that the company has ever managed to get anything done with the casual drug use that seems to go on around here. It does go some way to explaining how I've been able to get away with being such an imposter for so long, though.

"Me and some of the guys are doing a sponsored Go-Kart in a couple of weeks."

"Sponsored Go-Kart?"

"Yeah, at that place out by Warrington," he says, as though this'll mean something to me. It doesn't, a fact which I communicate to Kevlan or whatever his name is by shrugging my shoulders. "So, the guy who owns the place is letting us have it for free after he closes for the night, till he opens the next morning, and we're gonna do a twelve-hour non-stop Go-Kart session."

Again, the only response I am able to muster is a shrug of the shoulders.

"You know, for charity, like."

"Right..."

"So, we thought you probably wouldn't be up for it, like."

"You thought correctly."

"So... we thought maybe you'd be up for sponsoring us."

"I see. Well, the thing is, I sort of have a policy of not sponsoring people to do things like this. I may on rare occasions choose to donate to charity, but it won't be one that has solicited for me to do so, and I kind of think of this in that category."

He nods along with me, the blank look in his eyes telling me he has either not listened to, or failed to understand, what I've just said.

"Therefore I'm sorry but my answer to whether I'd like to sponsor you is no."

"Okay, cool. So, it's just that, well, we thought you might be into this charity, like, it might be a cause that's close to your heart, you know?"

I have to confess to being mildly intrigued by what cause people might think would be close to my heart.

"What cause might that be?"

"Well, it's for a local autism charity, so..."

"Why would that be close to my heart, Kev— I mean Dylan?"

"Well, you know, coz..."

"Because what?"

"Well, coz you're... you know..."

"No, I don't know. Because I'm what? What am I?"

"So, you know, you're, like, autistic an' that."

"I'm what?"

"You're autistic, yeah?"

"What the fuck are you on about?"

He takes a step away from my desk. "Well, you know, we all just thought..."

"You thought what? That I was autistic?"

"Well, yeah."

"Why the fuck would you all think I was autistic, Kevin?"

"Dylan..."

"Right, yes. Dylan. Why the fuck would you all think that I was autistic, *Dylan*?"

"Well, it's just, you know, the way you kind of keep yourself to yourself, you carry those cleaning sprays and stuff around with you."

I'm rubbing my eyes as he speaks, slowly counting to ten. "So you're an expert on the behavioural patterns of autistic people now, then, are you?

"Well, no, but I've seen 'Rain Man', so..."

"So?"

"And I saw that one with Sean Penn in, too."

"Which one with Sean Penn? 'Carlito's Way'? 'Casualties of War'? 'Fast Times at Ridgemont Fucking High'?"

"No, man," he says, as though I'm being stupid. "The one where he plays an autistic."

"I have no idea which film you're talking about. I'm not convinced it even exists. But I can assure you Dylan – and you can tell the rest of the lads this too – that I am not autistic. I do not have Asperger's Syndrome. I do not have Autistic Spectrum Disorder. I am not *on the autistic spectrum*. At all. Okay?"

"Yeah, cool, man. Sorry, didn't mean any offence or nothing."

"Well, I'm afraid you have caused offence. And I'm sure most autistic people would be slightly offended to think that anyone considered me to be one of them."

He pauses for a minute, scrutinising what I've just said, his look of confusion then turning into one of amusement.

"Ha, right, yeah. Nice one, man, like it," he says. "Right, thanks anyway Gary."

He leaves my office, still chuckling to himself. I watch through the glass in the door as he walks back into the main office to the rest of the staff out there. I see a few of them share looks of confusion as he presumably breaks the news of my lack of learning difficulty.

"Fucking stupid techy cunts," I say to myself.

I take the cleaning spray from my desk drawer and begin to clean my keyboard.

56

NINE

"He's… he's not an easy person to live with sometimes. In fact, he's not an easy person to live with most of the time."

"Few people are, Jenny," Michael replies, leaning back in his chair.

"No, I recognise that. And I've got my faults, the same as anyone else, but fuck me, Gary's hard work. I mean, *really* hard work."

"In what sense, particularly?"

"Well, his cleaning habits can be… oppressive at times. I know I shouldn't complain about living in a spotlessly clean flat, but sometimes I feel as though I can't so much as put a cup of tea on a table without him leaping up and putting a coaster under it or instantly wiping it up. I can't have a shower without him mopping up every drop of water I leave on the floor. If I'm cooking he's cleaning up after me – well, not even after me; he's actually cleaning up as I go. I put a pan down, he's already got it in the sink. I know I'm living in the cleanest flat in Liverpool, but it's all just a bit much."

"And what about his confrontational nature? His argumentativeness. Is that a problem?"

"No, not for me. He reserves that for just about everyone else he comes into contact with, but I'm exempt from it for the most part. And if he does that with me, well I can usually match him in that regard, to be honest."

Michael makes some notes as Jenny speaks.

"There's another thing too."

"And what's that?"

"Well, our sex life is… an issue."

"An issue?"

"Yeah, it's…" She trails off.

"It's okay, take your time," Michael reassures her.

"Well, the thing is, Gary wasn't very sexually experienced when we got together. He was pretty *in*experienced, frankly. It's not like I was Jenna Jameson or anything, but in terms of sexual confidence, we were oceans apart."

"And that was problematic?"

"Well, yeah. And it still is really. I mean, I know sex isn't everything, but it is important to me. And I want it to be important to Gary."

"And isn't it?"

Jenny gives it some thought. "I'm not sure how to answer that. I think it's more that he has no sexual confidence. He was single for a very long time. When he was at the age where most of us were out shagging, he was at home, suppressing the urge to even masturbate. The years where he was supposed to be developing a sexual identity, he was cutting himself off from sexual contact of any kind. And I think that, now, he just feels like he's too far gone to really embrace his sexuality."

"Do you have sex?"

"Yeah, it's not like we never do it, it's just that we kind of want different things from it."

"Can you elaborate on that, Jenny?"

"Well, I think the main difference between us is that I like to be spontaneous. I like to just do it when the mood takes me, for whatever reason, whether he happens to be looking particularly fit, or just because I happen to be feeling horny."

"And Gary doesn't like spontaneity?"

Jenny let out a little laugh. "Fuck, no. 'Prescribed', I think, would best describe his approach. Gary likes to know exactly when we're going to have sex. Like with most things, he has a certain routine he has to go through before we do it, otherwise it's just a no go. Which doesn't allow much room for spontaneity. No room, in fact."

"And when you do have sex, how is it?"

"It's… okay. I mean, I enjoy it, we both do. I just think we could both enjoy it more if Gary was less inhibited, more sure of himself."

"Mm-hmm. And have you encouraged Gary to be more exploratory?"

"Yeah, for ages I did, but it was clearly making him even more self-conscious, so I stopped."

"What about letting Gary take a lead, let him be the originator of any experimentation –"

"Michael, if I left it to Gary, we'd have sex once a month, at best. The need for me to constantly have to gently coax, subtly encourage; it's exhausting at times."

Michael notes the time on clock on the wall. "I'm afraid we'll have to bring things to a close there, Jenny. But we can pick up from there next week."

TEN

"Fucking autistic? Fucking idiots."

I'm muttering to myself as I head out of the office door.

"Fucking autistic. Fucking stupid techy nerd cunts."

It's only mid-morning but I have to get out of the building for a minute before I explode. I reach the street and just stand there for a minute, unsure which direction to even turn. I turn left and head up to the main road, and decide I could use another coffee. I reach the coffee shop and peer through the window, deciding that if there's a queue I won't bother. I see a couple of people scattered around tables, and look over to the counter and see The Knobhead behind it. He's looking back in my direction, his hands frozen in the muffin display. As I look over he slowly raises his hand and gives me a little wave. I go in and approach the counter.

"Oh, hey, man," he says, leaving the muffins alone. "Don't normally see you here during the day. I mean, I know morning *is* part of the day... I mean, don't normally see you here after that. Well, it's still morning, but... you know... later on?"

"No," I say. "I mean yes. I mean, I just need another coffee."

"Yeah, I hear ya, man, I hear ya. So what'll it be?"

"Coffee. Black."

"Yeah, kewl. You wanna try one of the guest coffees today?"

"Guest coffee?"

"Yeah, I've just put a couple of new ones out, man."

"Guest? Coffees?"

"Yeah, man. We're extending the range. We've got a nice Guatemalan blend that's proving really popular. Or there's the guest special."

"Guest special? So you've got a guest one, and a guest special one?"

"Yeah, the special is a little blend of my own actually. I've taken a Columbian and a Brazilian one and kind of put them together, yeah? They really complement each other well, you know?"

"How? How do they complement each other?"

The Knobhead squints a little and tilts his head like a Labrador that's been told to stay. "Well, the Brazilian has got a kind of hint of bitterness about it, while the Columbian is a bit smoother, yeah? So you've got the slight bitterness and the smoothness together."

I put my head in my hands and rub my face, taking in some deep breaths.

"Wow, you okay, man? You look like you really need that coffee."

"Yes, I do. I do need a coffee. Just give me a black coffee. Please. To take away."

"Sure, so you wanna go with the guest or the guest special?"

I can feel my anxiety increasing rapidly. I've entered a Kafkaesque world of hipster coffee shops, a world you can never leave, simply because there's so much choice.

"I don't know, just... what do I normally get? Where does that come from?"

"The one you usually get is a South American one, I think."

"Right. South American. Such as Brazil or Columbia?"

"Yeah, I think so."

I'm now on the verge of a panic attack. I'm trying to keep my breathing steady and measured, but I can feel it getting out of control. I can hear it too.

"Right, so give me that then."

"What, the special guest?"

"What?"

"You want the guest one or the special guest one?"

"What was the guest one again?"

"Erm... I'm not sure now, let me check."

"No! Just, just give me either. Please. I just need some coffee. At least, I *think* I do. Yeah, I do. Give me some coffee. Any coffee, I don't care."

"Right, yeah, kewl, man, here ya go."

He hands me over some coffee from somewhere in the Americas, and I take my card from my wallet. He looks at the card, a bit confused. "No bag today, huh?"

"What? Oh, right. No, I used it this morning. Contactless?"

"Huh?"

"Can I pay with contactless? On my card?"

"Oh, yeah, sure."

I tap my card against the screen and wait for the bleep. It's a sound I've come to welcome. Contactless technology is a great advancement in our civilisation, I feel. I've heard people talking about how it disconnects us, depersonalises the shopping experience. But that is exactly what I like about it. It minimises the interaction needed. The next step is for people to learn not to talk to each other at all, unless absolutely essential. No chit-chat, no small-talk, and absolutely no fucking "banter". The internet and modern technology have improved our lives in many ways. Again, people worry that it disconnects us, isolates us. Well, yes, it does. And I absolutely embrace that. Online shopping, contactless technology. Before long, these things will mean we don't have to talk to or deal with anyone unless we want to. Robots will eventually replace shop workers and delivery drivers, and they can be programmed according to customer's needs to talk to those who want it, and to shut the fuck up for those who don't. The stress of unwanted social interaction will be all but vanquished. As the technology develops further, we won't even have to carry cards, with the risks of them hosting germs to pass onto the skin. Eventually, our bank account details will be scanned via our retinas, and we will simply pass through a checkout without stopping, and our accounts will be debited accordingly. A brave new world, and I can't fucking wait. Amazon are already trialling exactly this kind of shop. Before long, they'll make it the norm, and I'll thank them for it. They can carry on cheating on their taxes and mistreating their workers all they like, as long as it means my contact with other people being reduced. The only worrying aspect is that the tech in question will most likely be being developed by weird pricks like the ones I work with.

I walk away from the counter without saying goodbye, and leave the shop. As I walk back to the office, I take a sip of whichever coffee it is I've been given and, fuck me, it's great fucking coffee. The Knobhead was right about the hint of bitterness, with the smoothness that follows. It also has a subtle natural sweetness to it. It really is amazing fucking coffee.

"Fucking bastard hipsters," I say, and hurl the coffee against the wall. As the cup bursts, sending its contents exploding against the wall like a poor approximation of a Jackson Pollock work, the smell of the coffee hits my nostrils; a strong caramel scent with an undercurrent of liquorice. It smells as good as it tasted. After a few seconds of internal debate, I turn around and head back to the coffee shop for a replacement.

ELEVEN

Tonight is Wednesday night. Sex night. Me and Jenny don't call it date night, because we're not going on a date. We're having sex, as we do every single Wednesday. During the early days of our relationship, one of the main difficulties was trying to align our very disparate sexual natures. Jenny likes sex to be spontaneous and passionate. I would probably prefer it to be non-existent, but as it is, I like to know where and when and how we are going to do it. It's the only way I can prepare myself for it.

In the early days, when Jenny would try and instigate sex, I was awkward and uncomfortable, afraid that my sexual inadequacies and inexperience would show. Which they did. Jenny did her best to encourage me, but the more coaxing she did, the more self-conscious I became. It wasn't that I didn't want to have sex with her; there's nobody on this planet that could get me half as hard as Jenny does, I just can't cope with the pressure of spontaneity. We eventually settled on this solution; one night of the week where we would, without exception, have sex.

Preparation begins straight after dinner. While Jenny goes into the bedroom, I take a shower. A thorough one. A really, really thorough one. As well as a solid all over body wash, I pay particular attention to my privates. After a good general clean of my penis, I take the shower head, pull back my foreskin, and turn the shower on as hard as it will go, spraying it directly onto my penis, all around the helmet, from a distance of about three inches. I turn the temperature down a bit, as the first time I washed in this way I left it on too hot, and slightly burned my bell-end. I then lift my penis up, part my legs and lean my top half forward slightly. This allows my balls to hang down freely, which enables me to aim the shower head at all sides of my bollocks, making sure they get a good spraying. Still in this admittedly ungainly and undignified stance, I then use one hand to pull one buttock to the side, and give my arse a good spraying. Nothing will be going on in that area, but it still needs to be clean.

I get out of the shower and dry myself with a clean towel as I walk towards the bedroom. As soon as I'm out of the shower, Jenny is on her way in. Once I'm dry, I get straight into bed. Jenny finishes her quick shower and comes into the bedroom, wrapped in her towel. She asks me if I'm ready, and when I tell her that I am, she takes off her towel, and stands, naked, at the foot of the bed. The sight of her naked, in these circumstances, is all it takes for me to start getting hard. She turns around and shows me her pert arse, then back around so I can see her perfect breasts. Once I'm fully erect, I take a condom from my bedside table and slip it on, and pull back the duvet. Jenny then climbs on top of me and we have sex, her on top throughout. This is the most effective position for Jenny to make herself come, essentially using me as a human dildo, which I am very happy with as it requires the least effort from me. She rides me gradually quicker, moving my hands occasionally to her tits or her arse, until she begins to orgasm. The sight of her face, contorted in pleasure, is all it takes for me to begin to come myself. We usually climax in unison, or very close to it, and Jenny falls on top of me, and we hold each other for a moment, before I get out of bed, take the condom off and wrap it in tissue, taking it to the bin in the bathroom, where I have another shower while Jenny changes the sheets.

TWELVE

There's an odd atmosphere when I arrive in the office, and not just the usual one of annoying hipsters chatting shit about whichever hilarious fucking meme they've just posted. There's a certain tension, one that isn't in keeping with the much-vaunted "chilled vibe" of the company, and one that is palpable even to someone as indifferent as me. I ignore it as I pass through towards my office, but I catch a glimpse of someone I haven't seen before in Eddie's office. Just the back of his head, but his baldness is enough to tell me it's somebody new. The lack of an elaborate fringe or vast, curly bedhead is a dead giveaway.

I sit down and go through my usual morning routine. I log onto my computer and begin working when there's a tap at my door. I look up and one of the lads, Lance I think his name is, Lance or Lenny or Lee, is poking his head round the door, as though using the door to protect himself from the objects he thinks I'm about to hurl at him for disturbing me.

"So Gary, meeting in the conference room, man."

"We've got a conference room?"

"Yeah, where we have all the meetings?"

"I thought that was called the Idea Factory. Isn't 'conference room' a bit... *conservative* for this place?"

"What? Oh, yeah, right... Idea Factory, man. Meeting in the Idea Factory, five minutes."

"And don't we call meetings 'Inspiration Assemblies'? You're not really adopting the lingo, are you?"

He looks a bit nervous now. "Right, yeah, we do. But I think this might be more of a normal meeting type situation. Anyway, five minutes, yeah?"

He begins to withdraw his head from my office.

"It's gonna be a quick one then, is it?"

"Huh?" Lance/Lenny/Lee asks, sticking his head back in.

"You said five minutes, that's a very quick meeting – I mean Inspiration Assembly."

He narrows his eyes at me, and his mouth falls open a little. "Oh, yeah, right. No, I mean the Inspiration Assembly is *in* five minutes." He begins to withdraw again, but sticks his head back in before it's halfway out. "I mean meeting assembly. I mean meeting."

"What the fuck's going on, L... lad?" I use the non-specific nomenclature as I'm not confident enough of what his actual name is.

He looks over his shoulder before whispering conspiratorially, "Someone's in from corporate, seems pretty big time, man."

My stomach makes an odd noise and tightens in an unpleasant way as he finally closes the door. I stand and pace around the office a little, wondering what this means for the company. Or, more specifically, what this means for me. I eventually head towards the conference factory, where I'm the last one in. Eddie is standing at the front of the room with the corporate guy. He's pushing forty, but has the type of body only successful people have the drive and/or money to attain, and then maintain; broad shouldered and muscular, without being a meathead, and wearing a casual looking T-shirt, which no doubt cost a week's wages for me, which accentuates his toned arms. His head is completely bald and apparently covered in some sort of expensive grooming product to make it shine like an orb, and he has the faintest hint of an exquisitely groomed goatee. His jeans are distressed and ripped but, again, look incredibly expensive. I look down to his feet, expecting a pair of ridiculously over-priced shoes, but, even more disturbingly, he is barefoot. I actually shake my head, before I realise what I'm doing and stop myself.

"Right, Gary, that's everyone then, yeah?"

This may be paranoia, but I swear the corporate fucker looks directly at me and raises his eyebrows, as if to say "*I* was kept waiting by *you*?"

"Okay guys, thanks for coming, yeah? Listen, I don't want anyone panicking, nobody needs to be losing their shit or anything, yeah? But this is Phil, and he's come up from London to erm... how can I put this... he's just here to –"

"Tell you what, Eddie," Phil butts in, cutting Eddie instantly dead with a voice that is simultaneously emphatic and friendly, "why don't I explain what I'm doing here? Is that cool with you?" He presents it as a question, but it's clear there's no room for discussion here. Eddie gives Phil the floor.

"So, what I'm doing here..."

Phil carries on talking, but I'm instantly distracted by his use of "so" at the start of his sentence. I haven't even been in the office fifteen minutes and it's the second time I've heard someone do that. On the average day at work, I'd estimate that roughly eighty percent of the sentences I hear begin with "so". And it's the same everywhere, overhearing conversations, on television, even fucking news reporters. When the fuck did this become the norm? When did this even become fucking acceptable? It's distracting, it's confusing and it's wrong. You might as well start a sentence with "but" or "then". It's infuriating, and it has instantly caused me to lose track of what Phil is saying. I tune back in to him – patrolling the floor as he speaks, making eye contact with individuals as he passes them, again in total control, but managing to still give off an air more of benevolence than malevolence.

"... and we love what this company does, which is why we want to see it reach its fullest potential. So the guys down at head office sent me up to just see what goes on here, observe, and see what we can do to help us all achieve our goals to the maximum degree. It's not a case of, 'Hey, Phil, go up there and sort these guys out, tell them what to do'. That's not what I do, it's not who I am. It's more a case of 'Phil, go up there, spend some time with these guys, understand what it is they do, and see what *you* can do to help *them* fulfil *their* potential. So – and I want to be absolutely clear on this one – I'm not coming in here with a sledgehammer, smashing things up. No, I'm here to nurture. Yeah, I'm an efficiency guy... that's a big part of what I do."

I dry swallow nervously at the word "efficiency", then nearly faint when I look down again at his bare fucking feet.

"But I also understand the creative mind, and the last thing I wanna do is come in here and stifle your creativity.

71

All I'm interested in is seeing who's reaching their top level, and who's... coasting."

Again, this might be paranoia, but I *swear* the bastard looks directly at me when he says "coasting", and the look in his eyes changes, I'm sure of it, for a nanosecond before switching back to his hip uncle routine as he walks past me.

*

Phil and Eddie wrap the meeting up a few minutes later and we all file out. I hear a couple of slightly worried mumblings, but mostly the mood is one of positivity; people seem to have swallowed Phil's benevolent routine unquestioningly, and are filled with enthusiasm by the prospect of the company moving forward, and of taking their work to the next level. As I close my office door and sit down, the only thing I'm filled with is the terrible feeling that, finally, I'm about to be found out.

*

Throughout the rest of the day I try desperately to put this morning's events out of my head. This is made incredibly difficult by the sight of Phil walking back and forth, the bright lights of the outer office bouncing off his trendily bald head and practically fucking blinding me. From my desk, I have a fairly direct view of his activities as he bounces around the place, introducing himself to people, shaking hands, taking calls on his mobile. I watch him "grabbing" a coffee, and effortlessly engaging a couple of workers in conversation as they come over to make themselves a drink. He shakes their hands, has them laughing and laughs with them. Cunt.

A couple of times, I'm certain I see his eyeballs rotate so that he can look at me out of the corner of his eyes. He's looking at me. I fucking *know* he is. He's probably been warned about me. He's probably wondering why, other than Eddie, I'm the only person here with their own office. He's sussing me out, the fucking prick. All this hanging around by the coffee machine, it's fuck all to do with being visible and getting to meet people. It's all a fucking show. He's come here for me.

THAT'S why they've sent him up here. Someone somewhere has complained to them about the freak who gets his own office, gets paid well for basically doing fuck all, who earns more than several people who actually have talent, who actually have something to offer this company, who at least understand what it is that the company does.

THAT'S why they've sent him here. For me. To sack me. To humiliate me. To expose me for the imposter I am. The complete charlatan I am. He's gonna strip me naked in front of the entire office and have them all laugh at me. He'll make me stand on a box, tell them to put a bag over my head and point at my genitals, give me the full fucking Abhu Graib treatment.

He's gonna drag me, with a noose round my neck, through the streets of Liverpool, and tell them all that I'm a fraud, and make them all throw stones at me, make them throw their slop buckets over me. I'll be like Christ on the road to Calvary, except I'll be carrying an ergonomic office chair on my back instead of a cross, a chair which had previously supported my spine, but now will crush it.

Instead of a crown of thorns, I'll be forced to wear a beanie of barbed fucking wire, and for me there'll be no Simon of Cyrene to help carry my burden. Instead there'll just be some bag-head, Simo of Smithdown, and he won't offer to carry my chair, he'll just ask me to lend him his bus fare then stab me in the eye with a dirty fucking needle.

Phil and his crowd will whip my bare legs as they follow me down to the docks, throw me on a raft and kick it back to Birkenhead, away from Jenny, who will join them on the docks and will also see, finally, what has always been evident. She will at last see what I really am, and see the terrible mistake she's made, and will turn away just before the Mersey ferry crashes into me. This is what Phil wants. I know it. The only efficiency this bastard is interested in is the most efficient way to ruin my fucking life. The most efficient way to destroy me.

He stops stirring his espresso and turns sideways and looks directly into my office, directly at me. I freeze as he does, as he stares right at me. A small smile crosses his face, and he raises his tiny coffee cup and nods at me. A nod that is no doubt his equivalent of the thumbs down from a Roman emperor. I look straight back down at my computer and pretend to be typing.

*

I try again to distract myself with work, or what passes for work in my office. I click on various hashtags, tag us in and retweet any that I feel may be relevant. I'm distracted almost immediately. Rather than scrolling through cultural or design threads, I find myself scrolling through the usual shite. The shite that has stopped me doing much work of any value the last few weeks.

I find myself looking at the profiles of many, many sad little men. Men who are very angry about multiculturalism, about leftism and "libtards", about immigration and refugees. Some of them hide behind anonymous avatars; some behind Union Flags or Pepe frogs. Some are open about their identity and have blue verification ticks next to their name. But all of them, to a man, share the same basic traits, the same anger about the same issues. I see them berating anyone who dares to contradict them. I see them attacking any celebrity who voices opinions that differ from theirs, telling them they don't have the right to comment on any subject other than what they do or did for a living, while simultaneously congratulating any celebrity who expresses opinions that they share, telling them how "red-pilled" they are.

For hours every day, every day for weeks, I look through these profiles when I should be working instead. These profiles of sad, angry, sexually inadequate men tweeting from their mum's house, or from their lonely bedsit, and marvel at the phenomenon. Having no online presence until I started working here, this was all new to me when I found it a few months ago. Of course, I was late to a particularly nasty little party that had been in full swing for several years, and I was stunned to discover that the whole world had now somehow become shaped by these people, these little boys who simply shouted loud enough and for long enough that the online world eventually began to listen to them. Then it began to follow them, then the ones following started shouting too. An online movement of lonely, sad, racist virgins who poured their self-loathing and dissatisfaction at their own station in life into blogs and vlogs, somehow used their computer keyboards and iPhones to seize control of a global narrative, spread misinformation, and essentially get a President elected.

They performed a global coup, armed only with a few factually inaccurate memes. The gun debate in America and beyond has become obsolete. Since working here, I've realised that there is no weapon more deadly in the modern world than a smart phone in the hand of an angry, inadequate white man. This is the side of the web that sucks me in, drags me down a rabbit-hole and takes up huge chunks of my day. When I finally manage to extricate myself from it, there's another side of it, less dark, but not that much less annoying: the *lad* side. This is a side of social media seemingly controlled by online betting firms. Through their Twitter accounts they keep young "lads" hooked with their recycling of existing "humorous" content; someone sliding down an escalator on a stag do and getting their nut sack almost ripped off, a photo of a drunk football fan seemingly having a shit on a stadium seat, and gifs and vines galore. *#lads, #bantz,* fucking Generation Y Tho. And, unsurprisingly, there is a significant crossover between these two sides. If they're not retweeting some Russian-controlled Brexit spambot, they're tweeting "shat on" to Gary Lineker's every post, telling various famous people they're glad their family died, telling them how shit they are, or trawling their timeline to find an old post that contradicts the sentiments expressed in a current post, at which point their mates will wade in, telling the celebrity in question how they've been "owned" or "schooled". But it's alright. It's banter. Just banter. And if you don't have banter, then

You.

Have.

Nothing.

And on the other side of the online aisle are the people who spend all day tweeting abuse at those on the right. Any gammon-like racist's every post, rather than just being ignored, blocked or reported as it should be, is greeted with similarly elaborate abuse, usually using what the abusers wrongly consider to be hilariously creative swear words. *Cockwomble*, *spunktrumpet*, *twunt*. For every Little Englander weirdo, there is an equally weird #FBPE account. Daily, this is a spider's web that, despite myself, I find myself voluntarily getting caught up in for hours on end, and by the time I come off, I need to medicate myself.

I look up from my screen and see that Phil has now gone. I've no idea how long he was standing there watching me "work", but I'm sure, however long it was, that he's already seen more than enough. I realise for the first time that my heart is pounding and my breathing is hurried. I reach into my desk and take out two plastic blister packets. I pop out a tablet from each and hold them between my fingers. After checking there's nobody watching me, I put them in my mouth and knock them back with a sip of water.

*

In the bogs near my office, I stare into the mirror above the sink, splash my face with water and wait for the effects of the tablet to kick in. Over the last seven or eight months, I have been gradually reducing my medication, encouraged both by Jenny and Kate, in consultation with a GP. In that time my morning Fluoxetine dosage has been reduced from 100mgs to 50mgs, while my nightly Quetiapine has been slashed from 300mgs to 75mgs. When I initially agreed to this, I panicked and went online to buy myself extra medication. Surprised that prescription anti-depressant and anti-psychotic drugs were so readily available, I purchased several boxes of Amitriptyline and Diazepam. It seems there are few prescription medications you can't buy online, either from here, America or the Far East. Add this to the fact that more and more people are self-diagnosing using search engines, and I imagine that within my lifetime GPs will become obsolete, and shortly thereafter the strain on the NHS will lessen as people simply die very quickly without correct diagnoses, rendering most of the debate around healthcare provision in this country moot.

The combined effect of my contraband meds is not immediate, but it's pretty quick, and I feel myself calming slightly as I return to my desk and get back on with my "work". My anxiety increases instantly, though, as I hear a knock on the door and look up to see Phil striding confidently into my office before I even have a chance to answer. Panicked, I inexplicably look back down at my keyboard and pretend to be typing, even though it's perfectly clear that I've seen him.

"Hi," he says. For reasons that are unclear to me, I pretend I haven't heard him, and carry on battering the keys randomly. I'm not sure if, on some level, I genuinely believe that if I just keep bashing away at the keys and pretending I haven't heard him, he'll simply go away, and never try to talk to me again. "Gary, isn't it?"

I stop typing and turn my head to the left. Phil has positioned himself at the edge of my desk. The lowness of my desk, and his height combined with the position he has taken up, mean that as I turn my head, I am staring directly at his crotch. I turn quickly back to my keyboard twatting, and wish I'd taken a larger dose of Diazepam.

"I'm Phil, good to meet you."

Now I clearly have to stop my bizarre charade and engage verbally with him. I turn my head again, and again am staring directly at the man's groin. I move my eyes up towards his face but, given my seated position and his vantage point, looking up into his eyes from this low down, it feels almost as though I'm gazing up submissively and/or adoringly at someone I'm giving a blowjob to. This, of course, makes me extremely uncomfortable so, in panic, I move my eyes back down to his groin. It takes me several seconds before I realise that I am now deliberately staring at another man's crotch, so I look back up at him as he looks down at me, looking like he's decided to simply face-fuck me to death rather than go through the ritualistic humiliation.

"Gary," I say, even though I know he already knows my name.

"Yeah. So Gary, I've just been going round the office, trying to quickly touch base with everybody, one to one, informally, you know. At the moment I'm just getting a handle on the place, that only usually takes me a couple of days at the most, then what I plan to do is sit down with everyone, individually, and get a handle on each person's key skill set, then work with them on what we can do to enhance those skills..."

"I have a very particular set of skills," I hear Liam Neeson saying inside my head. *"Skills that make me absolutely fucking useless to people like you."*

He keeps going, but I stop listening. All I can think is that if someone walked into my office now it would look like Phil was about to enter my orifice. I wonder whether he has chosen this standing position not only despite but precisely *because* it puts him in a position of dominance, and me in one of subservience. I wonder whether he gets off on making people feel uncomfortable in this way. When I caught him looking through my office window, he was probably sussing out exactly where he should stand to create maximum discomfort for me, and maximum dominance for himself. As I decide this is almost certainly the case, I realise my eyes have moved back down to his groin, and I've no idea how long they have been there. I look back up at him.

"... so if you can have a think about that over the next day or two, maybe put together a PDF which you can email over to me, then we'll knock heads again midweek kinda time and chew it over together, yeah?"

"Erm... PDF?"

"Yeah, or Excel or even Word, whatever's best for you. Okay, Gary, it was great to meet you," he says, offering a large but well-manicured hand to me. I take it after a slight pause, offering my usual weak handshake, and inadvertently allowing my eyes to fall, once more, on his groin. I turn them immediately back to my computer. He hesitates for a second before I hear him leave the room without saying another word. I very much doubt this cunt has ever left a room without an enthusiastic valediction before, so I'm convinced this means he has clocked me, at least once, staring at the area he allows only his wife and high-class escorts to cast their eyes upon. I know, beyond all reasonable doubt that even if he hadn't already made it his mission in life to destroy me, then he most fucking certainly will have now.

*

My anxiety powers my walk home, and I do it in less time than if I would if I'd actually tried to run it. I get into the flat and lock the door just as I feel a full-blown panic attack kick in. I drop to my knees, hyperventilating. I try to control my breathing as Jenny runs from the kitchen with a wooden spoon dripping with pasta sauce in her hand, presumably alerted by what must sound like a horse having a severe asthma attack.

"Gary, what the fuck?"

I try to alert her to the sauce dripping on the floor from the spoon, but I can't form the words.

"What is it?" Jenny asks. "What's happened?"

"Sau-sau..." I wheeze.

"Saw? Saw what? What did you see?"

I shake my head violently, my eyes now fixed on the trail of tomatoey sauce in a Hansel and Gretel-like path from the kitchen doorway. I point at it but she thinks I'm delirious, traumatised by the thing she thinks I've seen, so doesn't register what I'm pointing at. I shake my head again as she asks me what I saw.

"It's alright, you can tell me, whatever it is."

"Sau-sau-sauce," I managed to say.

"Saw us? Saw *us?* Who saw us, Gary?"

I punch myself in the head in frustration. Jenny, now becoming quite distressed herself, grabs at my hands to stop me, but in doing so, drops the spoon onto the floor, leaving a savoury blood splatter right next to her.

"Sau-sauce. Sauce... floor," I say.

"What?"

I stop hitting myself and take her head, and turn it slightly towards the floor. She sees at last what I'm trying to show her and stands up.

"Oh for fuck's sake, Gary," she says. "You're having a fucking panic attack about some fucking tomato on the bastard floor? I thought you'd been fucking raped or witnessed a murder or something."

I shake my head again, my breathing still not under control. "No. Sauce... made it worse."

"Oh. Right. Sorry." She kneels back down again. "I'll sort the floor out in a minute Gary. Just focus on your breathing for now."

I try to do as Jenny says, but all I can focus on is the sauce. Right now, even my impending evisceration at the hands of Phil is less of a concern. Even though the floor is tiled and will wipe clean in seconds, I want it sorted, but I'm immobilised. Jenny puts her arm around my shoulder and talks soothingly to me, trying to talk me down. With her other hand she rubs my chest and stomach. I close my eyes to stop myself staring at the floor. I focus on my breathing, the sound of Jenny's voice in my ear, the feel of her arm around me, her hand on me. She rubs my chest and stomach harder, and my breathing finally starts to slow. I put my hand over Jenny's and hold it as she rubs me. Suddenly, something unexpected happens. I feel myself getting hard. Jenny, intuitively, must somehow sense a change, because she slowly moves her hand down towards my cock. I grab it and shove it down there, and we jump at each other and kiss. Jenny clambers on top of me and I pull her closer in, but as I'm still kneeling, she upsets my balance and we fall over onto the floor, her landing on top of me, with me on top of the spoon.

"Ow!" I say.

"What?"

"Landed on the spoon."

Jenny reaches under me and pulls the spoon out, remnants of sauce still dripping. She looks unsure what to do with it for a moment before she moves it behind her head. I guess what she's about to do, and shout:

"Don't!"

But it's too late. Before the word is out she has brought her arm forward and released it, the spoon arching along the hallway, spinning as it does so, sauce flying in every direction, until it lands on the far wall and drops once more to the floor.

"SHIT!" I yell, and stand up. Jenny falls straight off me and bangs her head on the wall.

"Fucking hell, Gary!" she yells as I run to the kitchen and grab a packet of wet wipes. I run back to the hall and she's standing up, rubbing her head. "What are you doing?"

"I'm cleaning up the fucking mess," I say, starting at the splash on the far wall, and working my way along the splatter pattern back towards Jenny.

"Just fucking leave it!"

I stop and look at her. "Jenny. I can't," I say, my arms out as though she's made the most ridiculous statement of all time.

"Gary, come on, we were sort of in the middle of something there. Something quite important. It's just a bit of pasta sauce."

"A bit? It likes there's been a massacre in here. I've gotta get it, Jenny."

I kneel down and examine the wall, wiping every tiny drop with a wipe.

"Fine, I'm going to bed. I've got an early driving lesson in the morning. I've lost my appetite anyway," Jenny says, the double meaning of the word "appetite" deliberate, I'm sure.

I know I should go after her. I know that. I should leave this fucking mess and go and have sex with the woman I love, and talk to her about what happened at work. But I can't. All I can do is clean up, drip by drip. Which I do.

First I dab up the splashes from the wall with a damp cloth. It's imperative I deal with these first, otherwise there is a risk that they will stain the wall. Perhaps permanently. Fortunately, I have acted in time, and am able to remove them quickly and efficiently. Now I can concentrate my efforts on the more heavily soiled floor. Using some antibacterial floor wipes, as well as an antibacterial spray, I begin at the furthest point from the epicentre of the spillage, the kitchen door. Opening the floor wipes out, I wipe along towards ground zero, near the front door. Halfway between the two points, having become dissatisfied at the job being performed by the first wipe, I turn it over and continue. Spread open like this, a single wipe just covers half of the width of the hallway, so by the time I have worked my way up and back down, I have used only four wipes, which I think might be my most efficient ever use of cleaning product over the hallway or an area of equivalent size. I'm so pleased by this that I allow myself to use a wipe each for the skirting board on each wall, when I might usually have used one to cover both sides.

It takes me about half an hour to be sure I've got it all. I bin the wipes, then get in the shower, where I stay for forty minutes. When I get to bed, Jenny is either already asleep or pretending to be.

THIRTEEN

The next morning, Jenny has already dressed and left for work before my alarm goes off. I heard her getting up earlier, but I pretended I was still asleep, rather than deal with the fallout from last night. I still haven't learned how to confront and deal with relationship issues like this. In the grand scheme of things, I'm a fucking child at this stuff. If Jenny doesn't bring things up, then I will simply ignore them, as I have yet to develop the skills needed to amicably agree which side of the sink our toothbrushes need to be to cause me the least amount of anxiety, never mind how to talk through the fact that, last night, I made a clear and conscious choice to clean the hallway floor rather than to have what would have been only the third spontaneous fuck of our entire relationship.

Worse yet, I sabotaged the first spontaneous fuck that *I* had actually initiated. I wonder if this is how relationships end. Not instantly, even I know that. But I wonder if this, in relationship terms, is the first few dots of blood on the toilet paper that eventually leads to the diagnosis of terminal bowel cancer. I have no basis for comparison, but this feels like it could be fairly catastrophic. It occurs to me that the best thing to do might be to pack all my things together right now and move out. Just be gone when Jenny gets home. If this is the first sign of doom, the beginning of the end, then why prolong it? Surely it would be better for me to just fuck off out of Jenny's life right now and leave her the fuck alone to get on with her life than it would be to hang around waiting for the inevitable. Waiting for her to end up hating me far more than she presumably already does. Would it not be sensible just to vanish from her life, no screaming matches, no trial separation, not even a fucking note explaining my absence? She could just come back to the flat, see my keys on the table by the front door, then my empty wardrobe, and she'd know what I had done. She could simply breathe a sigh of relief, and get some sexually confident stranger from a bar to come round and spontaneously fuck her while she throws food and rubbish all over the flat, and not even bother to clean up after.

I decide this is the only course of action, and grab a bag from the wardrobe and start folding clothes. I'm stopped by a sudden stabbing pain in my chest. I sit down on the bed and realise that, even if I did leave now, I'd have nowhere to go. My old flat will now probably be inhabited by some forty-eight-year-old recovering addict and will stink of methadone and Pot Noodles, the walls decorated with mould and pages torn out of European hard-core porn mags. I don't have enough money to rent a flat on my own or to move into a hotel. That would leave moving back in with my parents as the only other option, and I'd rather drown myself in the docks than do that.

I begin planning out the fastest walking route to the docks, then throw my half-filled bag of clothes across the room. I look at the slight mess this action has created and instantly begin palpitating. I pick it up and put all the clothes away and get ready for work.

*

I'm over twenty minutes late when I get to the office. At least, I would be by any normal standard, but Eddie, unsurprisingly, adopts a far more relaxed stance when it comes to time-keeping than most company CEOs. He believes that structured working days are "way too restrictive" and that the team should "find out what sort of day fits them best, work around their creative sweet spots". My "peak" working time frame is one that allows me to get home at the most reasonable time whilst simultaneously allowing me the maximum time in bed. That's my creative sweet spot, Eddie. Even so, I don't think being late in the current climate is gonna do me any fucking favours. I don't want Phil getting any more evidence that I'm taking the piss, although stealing a living as I currently am might already be seen as taking the piss a tad.

I enter as stealthily as I can and slink past everyone, relieved that I seem to have avoided Phil and his chrome head. I nearly shit myself, then, when I hear his voice booming confidently out from the kitchenette as I pass.

"Gary, hi!"

I stop dead, my back to him. I consider just carrying on to my office, even though I've clearly heard him. I rock back and forth on my heels for a few seconds, unsure what to do.

"Erm, Gary?"

I take a few steps towards my office, then realise how ridiculous I'm being, and turn reluctantly to face him. He motions me into the kitchenette with a gesture of the head. I follow him in and he leans casually against the cupboards, spooning some watery looking yogurt into his mouth.

"How's it going, then?"

I don't answer straight away, as my attention is drawn irresistibly to the weird shite he's eating, and his bare feet.

"Gary?"

"Hmm?" I say, finally making eye contact.

"How's it going?"

"Oh, fine. Thanks. You?"

He gives a tiny smile, the kind you'd give to a thick child when they've given an adorably stupid answer to a simple question.

"I'm fine, thanks. What I was really driving at though, is how things are going in relation to what we talked about."

Again I fail to respond, my eyes again being drawn back to the yogurt he keeps spooning into his gob.

"Erm, Gary?"

"Yes? Oh, right. What we talked about..."

There's that condescending fucking smile again. It's barely there, just the slightest broadening of the lips. Probably not even noticeable to most people. He's probably not even aware he's doing it. But he is. I fucking know he is. My eyes move back to his yoghurt again.

"You ever tried this stuff?"

I shake my head.

"You should, it's fantastic. Absolutely zero fat, but it's packed with probiotics, high in protein. I eat a tub of this over the course of the day, and that's basically all I need, then a small evening meal. Wanna try some?"

I'm horrified to see him hold his spoon out to me, some watery residue dripping onto the floor. I want to tell him that there's very little difference between what he's just suggested and him whipping his cock out and asking if I "fancied a quick suck". Instead, I just respond with a meek "no thanks".

"Seriously, get onto it, Gary. It'll give you so much energy. Speaking of which, what we talked about..."

"Which was..?"

"You know, your PDF... you were gonna put one together for me, outlining your primary skills set, your core strengths and areas for enhancement."

"Right, yeah. Erm, I haven't quite got round to that yet."

He nods at me, clearly expecting me to elaborate on my reasons for failing to follow simple instructions. Simple to most people, anyway. After doing a few seconds of nodding dog impressions, he realises I'm not going to be forthcoming.

"Okay, well, if you can get that actioned for me – are you *alright*, Gary?"

At the mention of the word "actioned" my left eye went into an involuntary spasm. Office jargon always causes some sort of physiological response, usually something undetectable to most people, and I was hoping this response was also too insignificant to register with Phil. The added stress of the situation, though, seems to have ensured that this is not the case, and now that I'm aware he has seen it I can feel it getting worse.

"Yeah, I'm fine," I lie.

"But, your eye, Gary. It's... are you... can I get you some help?"

"No, I'm fine, really. It's just... an eye... thing."

"Okay, maybe you should get that checked out. You know, I bet it's dietary. You should really try this yoghurt."

I use the momentary distraction to begin backing away towards my office.

"So, if you could get that sent over to—"

"Yeah, I'll get that sorted," I say backing into my office, slamming the door and standing with my back against it, hyperventilating and twitching like a shit Bond villain, half expecting Phil to put his shoulder to it. I run to my desk and take my extra meds out and throw them into my mouth, chewing them dry and forcing them down. I pace around the office for a moment before I switch my computer on and sit down. I bring up Word and begin my first attempt to justify my position in a company that has been paying me a living wage for several months and getting absolutely fuck all in return. My fingers hover over the keyboard for a few minutes, before I give up without even having come up with a title. I stand up and kick my chair. It flies across my office on its casters and crashes against the wall. I look up and see Eddie is looking through the window at me. He opens my door, and I expect he is about the tell me to get the fuck out of his office, his eyes having finally been opened to what I really am by Phil, who has also probably put him through rehab to stop his judgment being clouded by the vast amounts of beak I still assume he does every day.

"Love that passion, man. Love it," he says, sticking his head in. "Never lose that."

He closes my door and walks away, shaking his head in wonder. This coked-up, sandal-wearing cretin is the only thing currently standing between me and financial ruin. And that is one of the most terrifying thoughts I have ever had.

*

"The fact is, Kate, I'm facing ruin. As surely as I'm sitting here, there is no doubt in my mind that within a matter of weeks, if that, I will be jobless, single and homeless. It's as inevitable as my brother's eventual bankruptcy."

"You use the word "inevitable"."

"Yeah," I say, "once his wife reams him in the divorce. I mean, I don't know if he was fucking anyone else or—"

"No, no, no," Kate interrupts. "I meant you use the word 'inevitable' in reference to yourself, and to your relationship with Jenny being doomed, your job being doomed. Is it inevitable? Is it not possible the outcome may be different?"

"No."

Kate does the therapist thing where they don't say anything and wait for you to break the silence. With Brian, I would sometimes just let the session time out rather than give in to it, but with Kate I'm actually paying for the sessions and, unlike fat, clueless old Brian, she does sometimes actually say things that aren't useless fucking tosh, so I relent fairly quickly.

"I'm beyond any other outcome now, Kate. There's no way out of it."

"But this is the first test your relationship has faced, and the first test you've really faced in your job."

"Exactly. And that's how tenuous my grasp on either of those things is. All it takes is one little question mark, and I've got nothing, no answer for it."

"Okay, let's look at each matter in turn. First of all, work. The evaluation you've been asked to perform, have you actually tried to do it?"

"I tried. I stared at my screen blankly for a few minutes, but I have nothing to offer. I've been found out. I can't write a report into how the emperor really *is* wearing clothes now that people have already seen his balls."

"Alright, so it won't be easy, but have you thought of networking with some of your colleagues? Maybe ask someone you're friendly... well, maybe not friendly with, but someone you can talk to – if you can see their report, and see how you can translate it to yourself? Or maybe searching online? I'm sure there are some templates available that you can use as a basis for—"

"See, these are all perfectly reasonable suggestions," I say, interrupting, "but this is advice that would only work if, first of all, I actually understood what my job role was, and I'm sure even you would agree that by now it's way too late for me to go and ask my boss what it is he's actually paying me for."

Kate reluctantly nods.

"Secondly, I would have to be on speaking terms with at least one of my colleagues, which I'm really not. I don't even know their names, most of them. And thirdly, I would have to actually want to save my job, which I don't."

"Don't you? Really?"

"No, I honestly don't. I *need* to save my job. I *need* the money, but I don't *want* to. And I fully realise that this puts me up shit creek, but I can't begin to motivate myself for this."

"Well let's put work to one side for the moment, and focus on your relationship with Jenny. From what you've described to me, it sounds like you've had a fairly low level row, and that there's some tension between you. What I've heard from you sounds like the kind of everyday thing that most couples go through on a regular, maybe even daily basis. Nothing I've heard sounds as though you're at or even *near* a crisis point."

"No, on this one, you're wrong, Kate. I recognise that for many, or most, the level of argument we've had is pretty small fry. But most relationships are founded on something more solid."

"More solid than what?"

"Well, as we've discussed before, I'm still convinced, on some level, that Jenny only ever really felt a bit sorry for me, and that she only stays with me because when she very quickly realised how fucked up I am she felt it was too late, and that dumping me would have made her feel like a terrible person, even though it probably would have been the right thing to do for the sake of her sanity. You've worked quite hard- on numerous occasions- to convince me this isn't the case, so let's not get back into that particular issue right now. But..." I trail off for a moment. "But there's another foundation that's sorely lacking."

Kate waits for me to elaborate, but senses I'm not able to. "What foundation is that, Gary?"

I stare at the wall for at least a minute, trying to form the words. "Sex," I say eventually.

"Your sex life?"

"Such as it is."

"Have there been difficulties lately?"

"Not just lately," I say. "Right from the start. I just can't... do it. And I don't mean that I'm impotent. I just can't... relax into it. I can't be spontaneous. I can't be passionate. I can't lose myself in the moment and just... fuck. It's not that I don't want to. I do, but it's not something I've done very much of, and it's not something that was ever important to me, or that I've been any good at. But I want it to be different with Jenny. I tell myself just to fuck her, just to enjoy it and let her enjoy it. But I'm so fucking scared of making a terrible mess of it, of disappointing her, of letting her down, that I play it safe and have trapped her in this awful routine of almost robotic sex. Although sex with a robot would probably be efficient, at least. And that, by doing that, of course I *have* disappointed her. I *have* let her down. And this is such a big part of what it all hinges on. She can put up with a lot of my shit, but why should anyone put up with that? Any normal person, anyway. Who wouldn't get sick of that?"

"I know it wasn't easy for you to say all that, Gary. This issue has sort of been the elephant in the room at our sessions for a while now, especially when we talk about Jenny. But having spoken about it now, how do you feel? Do you think you might be ready to have a conversation with Jenny about it?"

"Christ, no. In fact, I'm so far gone in that regard, and so much of a hopeless case, that, on balance, I really think it would be more straightforward to let things just... die between us. Let her take the initiative and finish with me.

Let Jenny dump me, let work fire me, and let me go back to what I was."

"What you were?"

"Yeah. Let me go back to being alone, in a little flat, on whatever meagre benefits are left available to someone like me, in some shitty part of Birkenhead, where I really belong. Not trying to pretend to belong in a world of relationships, living in a cool city, nice food, modern tech and all that shit. I'm a fucking fraud, Kate. I'm an imposter, and by now, I'm almost relieved that I'm about to be found out."

FOURTEEN

Phil is waiting for me when I get to work today. The second I get through the door the fucker ambushes me. He makes it look as though he just happens to be walking across the top of the stairs as I get there, spooning that weird fucking yoghurt into his gob.

"Oh, Gary, hi," he says as I try to slip past him. "Brain sesh in ten minutes, yeah?"

I have no fucking idea what he's just said to me, and thanks to his "yeah?" have no idea whether he's making a statement or asking me a question, so I stare at him blankly.

"In the main meeting room. See you there."

And he walks off, his bare fucking feet patting softly on the carpet. I go to my office and take out my Amitriptyline and Diazepam and knock back one of each. Then I take out another Diazepam and take that, too. I take a deep breath and walk round to the main meeting room. When I get there I'm horrified to see everyone sitting on the floor, with the chairs pushed back against the walls. Phil is sitting in the middle of a circle, one leg out flat, the other angled up towards his chest, with one arm draped casually over it as he leans back on the other. He looks as though he's about to do a photo shoot for a gay soft-porn mag which specialises in bald men, but has forgotten to take his clothes off.

"Oh hey, Gary, come in, grab some floor."

I nervously approach the circle and sit down as a couple of the other lads in the office shuffle apart to make some space for me.

"Now," Phil continues, "this is an open, informal forum for ideas, feedback and dialogue. I'm gonna be running these sessions once a week while I'm here, giving everyone the opportunity to talk about anything that's on their minds. Grievances can be aired as long as it's done with positivity, but we're looking for ideas, creative thinking and innovation. I want this to be as relaxed as possible, totally stress-free. Sitting on the floor like this puts us all on the same level, so there's no hierarchical structure, yeah? Everyone is the same as everyone else, and everyone's ideas are valid. We can take ten minutes or we can take an hour, depending on the vibe each week. So, does anyone wanna kick us off with any thoughts, any ideas?"

Phil looks around as everyone else looks down at the floor or around the circle, all waiting for someone else to speak up. He looks from face to face, weirdly nodding his head at the blank expressions, and after thirty seconds of silence, says:

"Alright, that's cool. Sometimes it's hard to speak up, it feels like there's pressure, yeah? I get it, nobody wants to say the wrong thing. But in the brain sesh, there's no wrong thing, all ideas are good ideas. You just need to relax more into the mind-set. I find taking my shoes and socks off at work helps that. The more physically relaxed you are, the more mentally relaxed you are. In fact, why don't you try it? Go ahead, take your shoes off. I think you'll be surprised how much it helps the energy flow through the whole body. Go on, try it."

There are some low-level rumblings of uncertainty as people look around the circle. I look across at Eddie, who looks at his feet as though waiting for them to instruct him on what he should do. Slowly, he reaches down and slips his trainers off, followed by his socks. With their boss having taken a lead, the rest of the group, to my horror, slowly begin to do likewise. Like the Jonestown settlers following their leader's instructions to drink the Flavour Aid, they all do a slow foot strip. But there's no fucking way I'm following suit. It's bad enough to have to look at a room full of hairy toes and untrimmed nails, but I'm not fucking joining in with this shit. I tense up as the smell of foot fills the room. I begin to breathe more heavily as I notice the bits of sock fluff stuck to people's toes. I see the dried, hardened skin on people's heels. I see in-growing toenails and verrucas. I nearly fucking gag as someone picks some fluff from between their toes and flicks it behind them. Eventually everybody in the room is naked below the ankle. Everybody except me. I realise they are all looking at me, waiting for me to flash some foot at them. I look up and my eyes meet Phil's. He's smiling at me, but I can sense the hatred raging underneath his soft countenance.

"Not joining in, Gary?"

"No, I'd prefer not to."

The whole room is watching us, wondering what will develop.

"You're sure?" Phil asks me, his voice friendly and encouraging, his soul full of resentment. "I think you'll

99

really be surprised how much it helps your creative thinking."

Yes. I'd be extremely fucking surprised.

"I'm sure."

"Okay, no problem. As I say, guys," he continues, now addressing the wider room, "this is an informal forum, so it's totally a 'come as you are' kind of deal. Whatever works for the individual, yeah? So, anybody feel like kicking us off, then?"

A lad with a shit quiff starts talking about the layout of some parts of the office, the "flow" of it, and I instantly zone out, unable to focus on anything but the couple of dozen pairs of rank feet surrounding me. The stench of vinegar and cheese grows in my nostrils. I can practically fucking taste it. It takes all my strength not to throw up. I try not to look at any of them, to focus on a fixed point on the wall, but in the corners of my eyes I can see them, shuffling around, criss-crossing over each other. I look around and I fucking swear these people's feet are fucking growing. Actually physically growing. What before were normal sized, if smelly, feet are now like hobbit feet. I clench my fists and breathe deeply, but it just makes me smell the feet even more, so I try to breathe only through my mouth, but that makes the taste even stronger. I'm about to run out of the room when I hear Phil speak up.

"Great," he says, "that was short and sweet, but very productive, I feel. Some really good ideas thrown out there, and as you relax more into these sessions I just know that it'll get better and better, week on week. Great stuff guys, really. Now, I'll let you all get back to work. Have a fab day, guys."

I stand up and head towards the door before anyone else has even begun to pull their socks back on. As I leave, I hear Phil's voice behind me.

"Gary, got a sec?"

Phil nods his head for me to follow him down the corridor slightly.

"Gary, I still haven't had your report yet."

He waits for me to answer, but I'm concentrating too hard on my breathing. Every time I breathe, the stench of foot makes me gag so I'm making a pathetic attempt to recycle what little oxygen I have stored in my mouth, which necessitates keeping my mouth closed. I'm unable to answer him.

"Soooo... have you... done it yet?" he says tentatively

I shake my head slightly, aware that my internal breathing is making an odd noise which Phil is clearly aware of.

"Any thoughts on when you'll be able to get that over to me?"

My chosen method of breathing, along with my growing sense of panic, is resulting in an increasingly bizarre noise, the epicentre of which is my throat. I make a vague shrugging gesture in response to Phil.

"Right, well, if you could get that actioned, then I'd... are you okay, Gary? Is there something wrong?"

Still I can't speak, so I raise a hand in an attempt to communicate my predicament with hand gestures, but quickly realise there is no universally recognised hand gesture that will convey the message "I am unable to breathe properly in case it intensifies the smell or taste of a room full of feet, a room which I have already vacated".

Instead, I simply point towards my face, then vaguely in the direction of the street. Phil follows the direction of my point, then looks back to me.

"Oh. Okay, I see," he says uncertainly. He clearly has no fucking idea what I'm trying to convey, and I'm unsure whether his pretence is an act of empathy or a further attempt to humiliate me. I decide it's the latter and run past him, down the stairs and out onto the street.

Finally I am able to breathe out, and slump, side-on, against a wall, desperately trying to catch my breath. I'm aware of footsteps behind me and assume Phil has followed me out. I don't turn to face him, and continue drawing in huge breaths. As I do so, I feel a cloth go over my mouth and an arm go around my neck. The cloth is soaked in some sort of chemical. I try not to inhale it but I'm still trying to catch my breath and can't help it. I feel myself weakening. I try to struggle against the arm round my neck as it tightens, but it's no use. The combination of whatever chemical I'm breathing in and the sleeper hold I'm trapped in is too much. I close my eyes, and as I feel myself losing consciousness all I can see are feet.

FIFTEEN

I wake up in darkness. At first I think I'm blindfolded, but as I blink my eyes, I realise that there's actually some sort of canvas bag over my head. It's not tight; it feels more like it has been placed over me rather than secured. Some light is penetrating through the tiny holes in the material and some from the bottom of the bag, so I know the room I'm in isn't dark. I also sense there is someone else here with me. I hear some slight movement in the near distance.

"Hello?" I manage to croak from my sore, dry throat. There is no response. I think about black and white images I vaguely recall of blindfolded men being shot in the back of the head in Cambodia or maybe Vietnam, and become very scared, which I probably should have been this whole time, but fear had given way to confusion and disorientation.

"Who's there?" I say.

This time I hear someone suppress a laugh. It seems I'm being toyed with, and I know what is going to happen. I am about to die. I will never see Jenny again, and will die not knowing why. As I realise this I begin to sob. I try to stop myself; I may be about to die but I'd like to do so with some small trace of the dignity with which I abjectly failed to live my life. I hear a small metallic click and imagine it must be the sound of a gun being cocked or loaded. I instinctively

103

put my hands up vaguely in the direction of my head, in a mixture of surrender and self-defence. I realise my hands aren't tied down as I'd thought they must be. I feel a hand grab the top of the bag, and it is lifted off my head. The light from the room blinds me, but I feel the person moving closer in, and hear the yell of a single, sickening word.

"BUCKLE!"

And I feel myself falling backwards off the chair as I faint.

*

I have no idea how long I was out for, but I wake up on the floor, lying on my side, the chair toppled over next to me. I lift my head up and look over my shoulder. I'm in a large, brightly lit room full of objects that, in my haze, make no sense to me. And, in the far corner, at a large desk, clicking at a computer mouse and sipping from a can of Stella, is Craig. He glances over at me and realises I've regained consciousness. He turns back to his computer and finishes what he's doing before he turns back to me.

"Alright, Gaz?"

"What?"

He gives me one of those looks he always gives when I've questioned something insane he's done, as though I'm the mad one. "What do you mean 'what'? It's a simple fucking question. Alright, Gaz?"

I push myself up so I'm now sitting on the floor. "Alright? Of course I'm not fucking alright."

"Why not?"

"Are you fucking serious? Why the fuck do you think?"

He shrugs his shoulders and takes another sip from his can.

"Craig, you fucking kidnapped me. You used some fucking chemical to knock me out and brought me... here."

"So? Anyway, it was only a bit of Dettol on the cloth, mate. Nothing harmful."

"What? Fucking Dettol?"

"Yeah."

"Why, Craig? Why fucking Dettol? Why any chemical?"

"Oh, I just thought the idea that you were being knocked out by chemicals might just make you a bit more... you know, susceptible, like. In case you put up too much of a fight for the sleeper hold. Which, obviously, you didn't because you're such a weak little fucking kitten of a man."

"Fucking hell, Craig, I thought I was about to fucking die!"

He laughs at me. "Who the fuck would wanna kill you, for fuck's sake?"

"I don't fucking know, do I? Someone who's fucking demented enough to kidnap me off the fucking street. Fuck me, what the fuck is wrong with you?"

"There's fuck all wrong with me. You're the one sitting on the floor crying."

"I'm not fucking crying, but I think I'd be entitled to. I thought I heard a fucking gun being cocked!"

"A gun?"

"Yeah, a gun. I heard some sort of metal clicking sound."

"Oh, that. That was just me opening a can, you bell-end. You want one?"

"NO I DON'T FUCKING WANT ONE. IT'S FUCKING MORNING. IT'S FUCKING MORNING AND I'VE JUST BEEN

KIDNAPPED. I WANNA KNOW WHAT THE FUCK YOU'RE UP TO!"

"Oh, don't make a fucking big deal out of it, Gary. It's not extraordinary rendition. I just wanted to see you."

"WELL WHY THE FUCK DIDN'T YOU JUST COME AND SAY HELLO?"

"I thought you might not wanna see me, so I decided to just... *bring* you here."

"What? Why wouldn't I wanna see you?"

"Why don't you get up off the floor, Gaz?"

Craig offers me his hand and I take it. He pulls me up and keeps hold of my hand, and shakes it, and pats me on the arm with his other hand.

"It's good to see you," he says, and pulls me in for a hug.

"Yeah, well it's good to see you too, Craig. Just... just don't fucking kidnap me, okay?"

"Yeah, alright. I wasn't planning on making a habit of it or nothing. Just a one-off, like."

I look around at the room and realise it's some sort of photography studio. There are cameras and other equipment over the opposite side, in front of what I think is a green screen.

"What is this place?"

He smiles mischievously. "Ah, your old mate Buckle has been a busy boy since he got out of prison, you know."

"Busy doing what? Are you a photographer now?"

"Well, you could say that, Gary. You could say that. Have a seat, mate."

He points towards an old bus seat that's sitting alone in the middle of the studio and we sit down.

"When I was in prison a lot of stuff happened."

"Oh, shit."

"What?"

"Well, you mean... did you get... you know..."

"What, raped? Nah, that doesn't really go on much to be honest. Cock lovers tend to just pair off with other cock lovers, and the rest of us, well, arrangements are made, you know what I mean?"

"Not really."

"Well, you've got a few hundred men all in the one space, no women anywhere, I mean, what do you think is gonna happen?"

"Well, I assumed rape."

Craig shakes his head like an adult talking to a dim child. "No, we just sort each other out, as and when. It's an act of necessity. You do each other favours."

"So, you had sex with men?"

"Yeah. Can you really see me going eighteen months without getting balls deep in something? Under any circumstances?"

"I suppose not."

"Exactly, Gaz. So what else am I gonna do? No quim, fuck a him."

"Is that an actual saying in prison?" I ask.

"No, made it up just then. Doesn't really work, does it?"

"Not really, no."

"What's up, Gaz?"

"I dunno. I suppose I'm just struggling with the idea of you having sex with men."

He bursts out laughing. "Oh, fuck off, Gaz! You're so fucking uptight and repressed you struggle with the idea of anyone having sex with anyone, you fucking fridge.

Speaking of which..." He throws the can into a bin and walks over to a large refrigerator, opens the door and I see that it's stocked full with cans of lager. "You sure you don't want one?"

"I'm sure."

He opens the can and sits back down. "Look, Gaz. I know your sexual values are somewhere between the Victorian and the Puritan but you really need to liberate your fucking thinking on this."

"What?"

"Sexuality, man. Times have changed. It's a lot more nuanced than you think."

"So, are you bisexual now?"

"Fuck those terms, mate. I'm a fucking sexual libertarian. Whereas you're a sexual librarian."

"What? What does that even mean? That I categorise sex according to the fucking Dewy Decimal System?"

"I dunno what the fuck that is, mate. Look, even if I believed in those terms, which I don't anymore, it's not that simple. Yeah, so I shagged a few blokes while I was in prison, that means nothing. Let's assume terms like gay, straight, bi or fucking whatever have any fucking meaning anymore, which they fucking don't, then what I did wasn't even within the brackets of gay or bi anyway."

"How? I mean, why not? If you're having sex with a bloke, then that's at least bi, right? I mean, the act itself is a gay or bi one, isn't it?"

Craig laughs at me so hard he spits his lager out. "Oh, mate. You're so fucking clueless, you really are. Listen, as I said, me shagging a few lads in prison was merely an act of necessity. You know what I'm like, I can barely go a few hours without shooting me gunk into or onto someone, so when you're talking months, there's no fucking way I'm gonna last that long. No fucking way. If you don't accept the reality of your situation and adjust accordingly then the only alternative is celibacy. Which is not an alternative for me. So I did what needed to be done. Plus, even within the confines of those narrow terms, there's... wiggle room."

"Wiggle room?"

"Yeah, fucking wiggle room."

"Craig, what are you talking about?"

"Okay, let me explain it to you as though I'm talking to some sad fucking weirdo who feels ashamed if he even gets a hard-on. Which I am. If another bloke sucks me off, then he's the one who's being gay, not me. Same if I'm doing a fella up the brown motorway. He's the one who's being gay."

I was shaking my head before he even finished his explanation. "Craig, I really don't think that's how it works."

"Yes. It fucking is. You, my repressed friend, don't get to tell anyone, anywhere, what the rules of sexual engagement are, capisce? And, like I say, those terms mean nothing to me anymore. But, if we are to recognise those terms, that is how it works. The giver is never the gay one."

I don't have the energy to argue with his definitions any more.

"So, you never..."

"Gaz, I will willingly and happily penetrate any willing adult orifice, should the mood take me. But nothing is ever going up my shitter. Except a tongue. And a finger. Maybe a couple of fingers. And possibly a small device of some sort, for the right woman."

My grogginess is beginning to lift, but the chemical taste in my mouth and throat remains.

"Okay, I think I'm pretty clear on your sexual mores now, thanks for that. Can I have a glass of water or something? For some reason, I feel like I've got chemical burns in my throat. It's almost as though some deranged cunt put a rag full of chloroform over my mouth in order to fucking kidnap me. Sorry, Dettol."

Craig stands and beckons me to follow him through the studio to a small kitchenette, where he fills a glass from the sink and passes it to me. I drink half of it down and use the other half to gargle and rub my face down with.

"So, this place, then," I say as I refill the glass myself, "you're... what? A photographer?"

"Well, I was about to explain that to you, Gary. I was going to tell you what happened in prison. The important stuff, that is, before you got fixated on where I've been sticking my cock."

"What important stuff?" I ask, finishing off the glass of water. "Were you gonna give me an insight into the best ways to make prison moonshine? Or explain the intricacies of the tobacco-based bartering system?"

"Oh, aren't you fucking hilarious? Listen, if you ever ended up in prison, you'd be passed around in exchange for about three fucking ciggies on a daily basis. By the time they'd finished with you, your arse would be so fucking loose they'd use their hands instead."

"I thought prison rape was a myth?"

"No, I said it's not commonplace. Besides, in your case, it wouldn't be rape. You're such a pathetic fucking weakling you'd simultaneously cry and shit yourself the second you got in there, and be so desperate for protection you'd be going round all the biggest, baddest lifers in there offering them your spread brown eye for their recreational destruction, just to get through your sentence."

"Well, it's a fucking good job I don't go round ripping people's noses off, absconding from the army and kicking shit out of coppers, and am therefore unlikely to be getting sent to prison any fucking time soon, then, isn't it?"

"Well I suppose it fucking well is, isn't it? Now do you wanna know what happened or do you wanna carry on being a snidey fucking cunt?"

"Alright, tell me your story, fuckanory."

"Thank you. Right, as you know, I was serving a fairly lengthy sentence at her majesty's pleasure, and as you can imagine, I was bored fucking senseless. So, unlike most of my fellow inmates, I decided to make use of what little opportunities for adult learning were available, as well as attending regular group and one-on-one therapy sessions. During those therapy sessions, there was one piece of advice that struck a chord with me. One of the counsellors who used to come in to talk with us said to the group, when we were talking about adapting to life outside at the end of our sentences and getting back into work and all that shite, he said to us, 'Find something you are good at, something you enjoy, and try to find a way to make a living from it.' Pretty fucking obvious, but still fairly sage-like advice, right? Now, around the same time, I'd been taking some basic I.T. classes in the prison library. And, as it happened, I had a natural aptitude for it."

"What, I.T.? You?"

"Yeah, trust me, I was as surprised as you are. As you know, I've never been one for modern technology. Never owned a computer or a laptop or a tablet. Never had the latest smartphone. I'm a proud fucking Luddite. Or I was, at least. But when I started taking those classes I was like Richard Pryor in that shit Superman sequel. Number three, I think it was, where he just turns out to be a computer whizz out of fucking nowhere. Always thought that bit was even less believable than some cunt flying around in tights, but it happened with me. Before you know it, I'm learning coding, programming, the lot. The librarian was ordering me all these advanced programming books. The rest of the fuck-witted, semi-literate no-hopers in there are struggling to type their own names and I'm learning stuff that'd get you clearance at fucking NASA. Well, maybe not quite that advanced, but you get the idea. I was fucking good at it."

"Wow. That's impressive," I concede. "So, if you were such a natural I.T. expert and the counsellor told you to make a living out of something you're good at, why did you become a photographer?"

"Well, Gaz, I was just about to enlighten you. See, although I have the knack for it, you have to consider that most banks or companies that use I.T. support aren't gonna look kindly upon me as a potential job candidate, not when you consider my lack of formal qualifications and history of violence. And even if they would there's clearly no fucking way that I'm gonna be sat in a fucking office for eight hours a day, wearing a suit, working with cunts and geeks. I wouldn't last five minutes without chinning some fucker."

"So..."

"So I asked myself what else I was good at, and how I could somehow combine that with my newly discovered tech prowess."

"And what else was that?"

I already know the answer before Craig opens his mouth.

"Fucking."

I nod my head resignedly. "Fucking. Of course. So you're a pornographer?"

"Don't fucking say it like that. Yes, I make pornography, big fucking deal. It's as valid a career choice as any other. And I'm fucking good at it too."

"Oh, I'm sure you are, Craig. So what's your specialist porn niche, then? I fucking dread to think."

"Gary... the term hasn't even been fucking coined yet to describe what I do."

"Oh Christ, it's something truly fucking abhorrent, isn't it?"

"Well, in a sense, yes. But..." He trails off, clearly struggling to find the words to describe whatever depravity he commits to camera. "Let me show you something."

He reaches into a drawer in his desk and pulls out a handful of DVDs and throws them at me. I catch some of them as a few hit the floor. I turn them round to look at the front covers; garish, lurid close-ups of fannies, anuses, mouths, cocks, jizz spraying in every direction. I nearly wretch at them, and at some of the titles; *Face Invaders*, *Speculum Surprise*, *Throbbing Gristle*, *Ram Raid*.

"Fucking hell, Craig," I say, throwing them vaguely back in his direction. "That's fucking horrible shit you're doing."

"Hang on a minute... who the fuck are *you* to tell someone their life's work is horrible?"

"'Life's work'? Craig, you've seemingly been at this whole pornography malarkey for a matter of months. And it's not work."

"Oh yes it fucking is, you cheeky little cunt," he says, standing up and grabbing one of the DVDs. "You've got no fucking idea how much time and effort goes into the production, filming, editing and marketing of these films."

He steps closer to me and waves the DVD box in my face as he emphasises his points. "This is a rarefied fucking industry, you sad little prude."

I catch a glimpse of the title on the box as he waves it in front of me. *Grumblecore 2: Piss On Me Tits Ya Bastard.* Rarefied indeed.

"Well I'm terribly sorry, there was me thinking you were just making cheap, sleazy, gonzo porn. I didn't realise how much artistry went into making..." I reach down and pick up a couple of DVDs. "... 'Supermarket Slags' and 'Birkenhead Bukkake'. I've clearly done you a disservice. This is some fucking highbrow stuff you've got going on here."

Craig looks genuinely hurt, then steps closer to me and smacks the DVD out of my hand. He leans in close, and I worry that he's going to inflict some physical harm on me. Something which, despite the disruption and trouble he's caused me, has never happened before.

"Right, you little fuck. That's the last time I'll allow you to slag off my work. One more snidey fucking remark and

I'll be making a fucking snuff movie. With you in it. You understand me, you fucking shithouse?"

"Yeah, alright. Sorry," I say, fully believing his threats. He takes a deep breath and seems to calm down a little before removing his face from the vicinity of mine.

"Alright, some of my early titles were a bit... raw, I suppose. But that's what I'm trying to tell you. I wanted to do more than that. I was making money, which isn't that easy to do in porn these days, trust me. I managed to do okay out of it by using social media and things like that to give my company a different sort of identity compared to most. But making money wasn't ever really my main aim. I just wanted to do something I enjoyed and was good at. But I realised that, after what had happened to me, after I'd been given another chance, I realised I wanted to somehow use what I had to help others."

"So you stopped doing porn and started making educational films for adults just out of prison?"

"No, you prick. But, actually, you're not *that* far off with the second part."

"What, really?"

Craig thinks for a moment. "Well, no. Not really, but... sort of." He sits back down at his desk. "Look, I was thinking, what if, by having an audience, and let's face it, there's probably a certain type of person who watches the sort of porn I was doing. Male, obviously, single, not particularly well educated. But they're my audience, for better or worse. Mostly worse. But as they're there, watching my stuff, what if I could somehow open their eyes to other things? To things more fulfilling than wanking their tiny, half-flaccid cocks into a sock in some lonely fucking bedsit before crying themselves to sleep?"

"So you started making educational porn?"

"In a way, yeah. Educational porn. Porn with a social conscience. Call it whatever you want."

"How did you do that?"

"It's surprisingly easy. See that over there?"

I turn my head in the direction Craig is pointing. In the far corner is a clear screen.

"You know what that is, don't you?"

"It's a green screen, right?"

"Exfuckinzactly! It's a green screen! And with that, I can put me and my other performers anywhere in the world, at any time in history. And while my audience of inadequate basket cases are grunting away over their laptops or smartphones, they're also learning about social issues or historical periods they'd otherwise probably never have heard of."

"Okay. Like what?"

Craig thinks for a moment. "Well, a few months back I shot a short film that used the French Revolution as a backdrop. Thirty minutes or so of hard-core fucking, but the viewer also got to learn about King Louis, Marie Antoinette, the uprising, all that stuff."

"And what was that particular cinematic marvel called?" I ask, instantly regretting it.

"'Let Them Eat Cock'," Craig says, shrugging as though it's the most obvious thing in the world. "Honestly, Gaz, thanks to that screen, it's a piece of piss. Once you've got that and some willing performers, all you need's a few costumes and props. Speaking of which, you're sitting on one of my props now."

I look down at the bus seat I'm sitting on and realise that, rather than the hipster affectation I thought it was, it's something that has, at some point, been covered in the sexual secretions of Craig and fuck knows who else. I quickly stand up, and Craig laughs as I check myself for spunk stains.

"Don't worry," he says, "I wiped it down afterwards."

"Oh well, that's very fucking reassuring. What the fuck did you use a bus seat for, anyway?"

"I filmed a scene based around the Rosa Parks protest on the bus. One of the best things I've done, actually."

"For fucks sake, Craig. Did it not occur to you to tell me what you'd been up to on that chair before I fucking sat on it?" I ask as I move over to a large leather chair that looks like it was salvaged from an old fashioned gentleman's club.

"No, to be honest. I mean, just about every piece on furniture in here has been fucked on at some point."

I stop just before my arse comes into contact with the leather of the chair and stand back up. "Look, Craig. I'm not being funny, and it is good to see you, and I'm glad you're doing... well... this." I gesture towards the pile of DVDs. "But, how did you find me? And why?"

"How? Gary, I've just told you, I'm a fucking computer whizz now. I'm like the mad fucker off. 'A Beautiful Mind' crossed with that Wikileaks cunt. Only I'm not a fucking rapist shut-in like he is."

"But, I've got practically no personal online presence, I'm not on Facebook, I'm not on Twitter, I'm not—"

"Gary, this is 2020. There's no fucking hiding place anymore. Trust me, if you exist, people like me can find you, should we so wish. And besides, you've moved from Birkenhead to Liverpool, it wasn't exactly fucking challenging. If you'd moved to a log cabin in British Columbia, I'd have found you."

"Okay, so that's the how. But why? Why now?"

"Because I think you need rescuing, Gary."

"What? Rescuing? From what?"

"This fucking life you've got yourself into. The happy home, the cushy fucking corporate job. You've fucking sold out, mate."

"Sold out? How the fuck have I sold out? I never had any fucking principles in the first fucking place, so how the fuck have I sold out?"

"Come on, Gaz. Look at where you work, where you live. Look at your fucking suit."

I gesture at my shirt. "I'm not wearing a fucking suit, Craig."

"Yes you fucking are, Gary. A suit of normality. This isn't you. You're not happy. I can tell."

"Not happy? Well that's a ground-breaking theory, Freud. When the fuck have I ever been happy?"

"This is different, though. Gary, I think you need me in your life. You need your old mate Buckle."

"NO! I fucking don't need Buckle. Craig, I'm glad to see you. Sort of. But I don't wanna see Buckle."

"But Craig is Buckle. Buckle is Craig."

"Stop fucking talking about yourself in the third person! It's weird. Look, Craig. I'm gonna have to go. I was at work when you dragged me off the street. They're probably wondering where I am."

"Doubt it."

"Well, fucking Phil probably is."

"Phil?"

"Yeah. He's some fucking efficiency expert fucker. The cunt's gunning for me, I know he is."

"Phil, you say?"

"Yes, Craig. Phil."

"Okay, you'd best get back, then, I suppose."

"Where the fuck am I anyway?"

"You're just a few streets down from your office."

"What?"

"Yeah. Just go down the stairs. You'll recognise where you are right away."

"Right. I'll see you then."

"Will you? I mean, are you gonna come back and see me?"

"I dunno. Yeah, probably. I don't know when, though. I've gotta get this Phil fucker off my back first."

"Right, I'll see ya, then."

"See ya, Craig."

I let myself out and head down the stairs onto the bustling street outside.

*

When I get back to the office, Phil is passing by the top of the stairs as I run up them, trying to look as though he just happened to be passing by as I arrived. Like fuck he was. The baldy fucker has obviously been waiting for me.

"Gary, you're back."

He doesn't miss a trick, this efficiency expert. I reach the top of the stairs where he is waiting for me, his feet still flagrantly naked.

"Anyway, Gary," he continues, "as I was saying before you left, if you could just get that evaluation done and pop it over to me, I –"

He stops midsentence and sniffs the air between us.

"Gary, there's a... smell. Is it coming from you?"

I realise the Dettol Craig used to subdue me is still clinging to me, and is quite pungent. "Oh. Yeah. It is."

"Do you mind me asking what it is? It's very strong, Gary."

"Erm. It's... just... chemicals."

"Chemicals?"

"Yeah. I've... got some chemicals on me. It's no big deal."

Phil places the tiny espresso cup he's been sipping from on a nearby table and takes a step closer to me. I instinctively step back, but bump straight into a wall. He puts a hand on my shoulder.

"Gary," he says earnestly, "if you have a substance abuse problem, then we can help you. The company has access to a very good clinic. You don't need to be alone in this struggle, but you need to ask for help."

"What? No, you've got the wrong end of the stick."

"Gary, I had the wrong end of the stick for six years before I finally grabbed the right end of the stick and sought the help I needed."

"Eh?"

"Look, I know the signs. I've seen them before. You're shaking."

I follow his eyes to my arm and see that he's right. I am indeed shaking, or at least my arm is. Far from being caused by drug or alcohol withdrawal, however, it is caused by the discomfort at having Phil's arm resting ever so fucking tenderly on top of it. I slide along the wall away from his touch, and he lets his hand drop back to his side.

"Phil, really, I'm not an addict. It's a long story, but I just got some chemicals spilt on me."

He nods and exhales slowly. "Okay, Gary. I'll take your word for it, but I'm gonna be honest with you here, I'm not a hundred percent convinced. If you're withholding, then I understand why, and if and when you're ready to seek help, I'll be there."

His countenance darkens slightly, and portrays a hostility I've previously been sure was there, but hadn't yet seen.

"If you're telling the truth, however, then there's no reason why you can't have your self-evaluation ready for me, is there Gary?"

I shake my head pathetically.

"Great. Shall we say you'll have it done by the end of the day on Thursday?"

He doesn't wait for a response because he wasn't really asking a question. As he walks away I realise what a great opportunity I've just missed. If I'd said I was a crystal meth and coke addict I could have bought myself at least a few weeks of respite. He probably would have forgotten all about me and been called back to head office by then, sent off to humiliate and degrade some other poor, out-of-their-depth fucker. I smack myself in the face for my stupidity, as I watch Phil walk into the kitchen, and take another tub of his fucking yoghurt from the fridge. He turns around and looks me straight in the eye as he spoons it into his mouth, before disappearing from view. I realise that the rules of engagement have just changed. Hostilities have escalated.

SIXTEEN

I stand outside the flat for a full ten minutes before I finally put the key in the door. When I enter I expect there to be no lights on and a deathly silence, so I'm surprised to find the hallway light on and the sound of the latest She Drew the Gun album coming from the bedroom. Although better than the sounds of silence I was anticipating, this is also a change in the usual protocol. There are no cooking smells and no sound of Radio 6 from the DAB radio in the kitchen. I stand in the hallway for a moment, unsure whether I should interpret this change in routine as a fuck off. I decide I need to leave the flat and walk around the block for ten minutes, and see whether normal order has been restored by the time I return. My hand is on the door handle when Jenny emerges from the bedroom, wearing one of her smarter "going out" dresses. She looks fantastic.

"Get ready," she says as she crosses the hallway into the kitchen.

"Get ready? For what? Nuclear annihilation?" I say, following her in.

"No, we're meeting your mum and dad for dinner."

"On balance, I'd probably prefer nuclear annihilation."

"Very funny."

"Who's joking? Since when are we meeting my parents? Who arranged this? And for what reason?"

"Me and your mum arranged it. She rang me at work today and invited us out."

"And you accepted? Without either of you consulting me?"

"Of course I accepted. Why wouldn't I?"

"BECAUSE THEY'RE MY PARENTS! WHY *WOULD* YOU ACCEPT?"

"Gary, it's no big deal. We're going for dinner. It's not like we would have had other plans, is it?"

"Jenny, you know full well it's a big deal to me. Don't be obtuse."

"Obtuse? You're fucking calling *me* obtuse?"

I realise I'm on cracking ice here. One wrong word and I could well be up to my arse in freezing water, so I adopt the most diplomatic tone of voice I can manage.

"No, I didn't *call* you obtuse, I told you not to *be* obtuse. There's a significant difference."

She turns to face me, and takes a few steps towards me, until she's practically squaring up to me. "Don't get into fucking semantics, Gary. Telling me not to be obtuse *implies* that I'm being fucking obtuse. Which I was not."

I realise my attempt at a tone of diplomacy was about as diplomatic as Idi Amin after a meth binge, and that if I continue along this path no good will come of it. So I apologise, accept that I'll have to dine with my parents tonight, and go and get in the shower.

*

We get to the restaurant just after eight. It's yet another new place in town, all bare brick and metal pipes on display.

"It's a bit fucking hipstery, isn't it?" I whisper to Jenny as we stand at the hostess station. "If they serve chips in one of those fucking basket things then I'm fucking leaving. I'm not kidding."

"Well you could always try ordering something other than fucking chips for a change, couldn't you?" she whispers back, angrily.

"I like chips. And these probably only do quadruple-cooked, skin-on chips with a delicate seasoning, so it'll be different from the chips I normally have."

"For fuck's sake, Gary," Jenny says, now no longer whispering, "can you at least try not to be an obstreperous fucking cunt?"

"Erm, can I help you?"

A nervous looking young woman with an Eastern European accent is standing in front of us, presumably wondering whether she's going to have to call the police.

"Yeah, sorry," Jenny says, composing herself. "We're meeting someone. The name's Lennon."

The woman checks the reservations book, her eyes flicking up at us occasionally, seemingly glad to have the counter between us for protection. "Ah, yes, Lennon, eight o'clock. Your friends are here already. If you'd like to follow me..."

We follow her and her incomplete sentence past several booths until we see my parents. Mum is looking at the cocktail menu and Dad is fiddling clumsily with what I think is some sort of postmodern salt shaker. He's also looking around at the decor, apparently even more out of his element than I am.

For the first time, I notice that he looks old. I mean, he's always seemed old to me but now he genuinely looks as though time is catching up with him. His hair is much greyer and thinner than I'd realised, his skin a bit rougher, well, as rough as it can be on a man who spent his entire working life sheltered from the elements in classrooms. Most state schools may well be ramshackle fridges but that doesn't compare with working outside all day. Even so, although it could be the lighting in here, his skin looks rougher than I'd realised.

Placing the shaker back down on the table and folding his hands uncomfortably on the table, he looks out of place, and running out of time. I'm struck with the realisation that having to put up with me as a son for the last thirty years has probably caused him to age at more than the usual pace, as has dealing with Tory Boy Ben for even longer. I feel sorry for the old sod, especially as he'll also have to put up with my mum being pissed as a fart on expensive cocktails, if her whoops of delight as she points out some extravagant bevvy she's found are anything to go by. His plight is so desperate that he actually looks pleased when he looks up to see me.

"Gary!" he says, practically leaping up to greet us. He gives me a quick handshake and pretends not to notice me wiping my hand as he gives Jenny a peck on the cheek. Mum turns and waves excitedly and beckons Jenny to sit down next to her.

My mum and dad fucking love Jenny. Of course they do. How could they not? Never in a million years would they have imagined me having a girlfriend. Never mind one as beautiful and intelligent as Jenny. The fact that she has a good job with very decent pay is the icing on the cake, as they are no doubt convinced it's only a matter of time before I fuck my own job up somehow. Of course, it's looking as though they'd be right on this point.

I sit down next to Dad as Mum shoves the cocktail menu in Jenny's face. "Will you be joining me in sampling a few cocktails, Jenny?"

"Yes, I think I will, actually," Jenny says, looking over at me.

Mum follows her gaze to me and gives me a disapproving look. I only just manage to stop myself flicking the Vs at her, before she and Jenny peruse their options. Dad gives me a slightly more sympathetic "uh-oh, someone is in the doghouse" type look as he hands me the food menu.

"How's work?" Dad asks.

"Fucking atrocious."

"Oh."

He slams the menu shut, seemingly having made up his mind in seconds. Mum waves a waiter over and orders a jug of some elaborate sounding cocktail, and me and Dad order a beer. I continue to peruse the menu as a luminous, fruit-filled monstrosity is placed down on the table and two vast glasses of it poured for Mum and Jenny. My mum takes a big gulp of it.

"Ooh!" she says. "It's a bit strong, isn't it?"

"A bit, yeah... bit on the sweet side too," Jenny says, grimacing.

"Mmm, I like that, though," Mum says, taking another big gulp. "Can't taste the alcohol as much."

"No," Jenny says as Mum tops her own glass back up. "You can definitely still taste the alcohol."

The waiter reappears with his notepad in his hand. "Hey, guys, we all ready to order?"

Everyone orders their food. I go for the simplest burger on the menu, the only one that doesn't appear to come with several layers of topping, and Mum asks for a jug of a different but equally strong sounding cocktail.

"So you two," my mum says, her voice already starting to slur a little, "what news have you got for us?"

I realise that, having been invited out by Jenny, she has got it into her head that maybe we had some significant news. She must have imagined that either we're getting married or that Jenny is pregnant. The strong cocktail she's helped Mum demolish perhaps should have disavowed of the latter notion, but then again Mum does belong to the generation that probably thought heavy alcohol intake and smoking were beneficial to a foetus.

"Nothing," I say quickly, keen to remove any ambiguity and hope from the situation. Mum's face sinks a little, though she tries to hide her disappointment, and I'm certain I detect a glimmer of resentment in her eyes. As though to confirm my suspicions, she turns away from me and engages Jenny in an entirely separate conversation.

"Sorry", I feel like saying to her, *"next time we meet I'll be sure to have ejaculated inside Jenny with sufficient velocity to impregnate her, purely to please you."*

I can't believe she'd actually be stupid enough to think I'd be a suitable candidate for parenthood. She's seen the horrible little bastard my brother produced, and he actually *wanted* to be a father. If Thomas is anything to go by, the Lennon seed should be wiped from the face of the earth.

Our food arrives, and I'm unsurprised but no less horrified to see that it is served on what I think are roofing tiles, with my chips not in a mini metal basket but, of all fucking things, a clog. An actual, real life, wooden clog. The chips inside it look genuinely excellent, but the sight of the clog makes me want to cry or flip the table over. The waiter walks away, telling us to enjoy our meals, which I may now find very difficult.

"What about this place, eh, Gary?" Dad says. "Bit fancy, isn't it?"

"Fancy? It's not fucking fancy, it's fucking ridiculous, Dad," I say, gesturing at my meal.

"Don't speak to your father like that," Mum hisses drunkenly.

"Like what?"

"Like, like *that!* Like a bloody... smart-arse!"

I can't help but laugh, which doesn't go down well with either Jenny, who scowls at me, or my mum.

"Don't laugh at me, Gary!"

"Had a drink, have you, Mum?"

"Yes I've had drink. I'm entitled to a drink, aren't I?"

"By all means, drink yourself into a fucking stupor if you want, but if it's gonna make you kick off at me over an innocuous comment then maybe you should take it easy."

"Alright, everyone," Dad says gently, "let's not argue, eh? Let's enjoy our meals, shall we?"

As he says this, he looks down at his clog, picks up his fork, and awkwardly tries to negotiate his chips out of it. I pick mine up and tip the chips onto the slate. We all eat in tense silence for a few moments, until the waiter bounds enthusiastically back over.

"Hey guys, everything okay with your meals? Can I get anyone anything else?"

"Yeah, actually," I say, "can I have some mayonnaise?"

Jenny looks up from her plate and glares at me, no doubt mindful of the Lark Lane incident, and probably silently praying that they actually have some mayo. There is a very tense, very long-feeling moment before the waiter responds.

"Sure," he says, and Jenny's shoulders un-tense and she looks back down at her pulled-pork burger. "Garlic or chilli?"

"What?"

Jenny's eyes are straight back on me.

"Can I get you some garlic mayo or chilli mayo?"

"Just plain. Plain mayonnaise."

"Oh, I'm sorry," he says, "unfortunately we don't have plain mayo, just garlic or—"

"Or chilli, yes, I gathered," I interrupt, putting my head in my hands.

"Gary..." Jenny says, now no longer as confrontational as her initial glare suggested, now more placatory. But it's too late.

"So you don't have, anywhere in the building, a single jar, bottle, or sachet of ordinary, plain mayonnaise, is that right? Not one? Anywhere?"

"I'm sorry..." The waiter takes a step away from the table. "We don't. Erm, just gar—"

"GARLIC OR FUCKING CHILLI!"

"GARY!" Jenny, Mum and Dad all shout in chorus.

"What? Fucking Gary what? Why is it too much to ask to be able to go into a restaurant and get some fucking mayonnaise? Why must that be so fucking difficult? I'm not asking for rare truffles. I'm not asking for a fucking dodo egg, it's fucking mayonnaise, for fuck's sake! It's a standard fucking condiment. And why can't I eat from a fucking plate anymore? I mean, look at this shit! Roofing tiles? A FUCKING CLOG?"

I stand up and shove the tiles and clog onto the floor, scattering my triple-cooked chips everywhere, and the waiter takes another step back to avoid getting covered in mayonnaise-free food. He finally scurries away to alert either his manager, the police, or both.

"WHAT THE FUCK IS WRONG WITH THIS COUNTRY? WHAT THE FUCK IS WRONG WITH THIS PLANET?"

Dad is tugging at my sleeve, trying to calm me down. Mum is simultaneously downing her cocktail and crying, which is one of the strangest things I've ever seen, and Jenny looks like she wants to kill me. Instead, she stands and throws what remains of her drink in my face.

"Did you just throw a fucking cocktail over me?"

"YES! TO TRY AND GET YOU TO CALM THE FUCK DOWN!"

"Why would that calm me down? It's fucking disgusting. It's like being covered in sugary ectoplasm."

"Well, that's what people do to hysterical people sometimes, isn't it?"

"In a fucking Richard Curtis film, maybe. Fucking hell. Did you honestly think that would work? On me of all fucking people? I'll need a fucking shower now!"

"Well, seeing as we're obviously gonna have to leave now, before we get fucking arrested, that won't be a problem. Jan, I'll call you. Paul, I'm sorry."

"Don't fucking apologise for me!" I shout.

"Well somebody fucking has to, don't they? You're obviously not going to do it for yourself."

"Fine, let's go."

We both pick up our coats and head towards the door.

"So, how do you feel that went?" I say.

*

The taxi ride home is inevitably tense, even the jovial cabbie sensing it and wisely aborting initial attempts at conversation. When we arrive at the flat Jenny gets out without a word and leaves me to pay the driver.

"Uh-oh," he says, nodding in her direction as she walks towards our building. "Looks like you're in trouble there, mate."

"Mm-hmm." I count out the fare, and although I'm looking down at my palm I can sense him leaning in closer to me.

"Might have to give her a good seeing-to, my mate, heh-heh-heh."

"FUCK YOUR OWN DICK!" I yell, as several possible angry responses collide in an inarticulate outburst.

"Fuck me what?!" he responds, not sure whether to laugh, take offence or simply twat me.

"You fucking heard me," I say as I throw a tenner at him and get out of the cab.

I consider using my lame attempt at defending Jenny's honour to offset the shit-storm I have caused, but quickly decide against it when I enter the kitchen to see her not standing with a large knife ready to quite justifiably disembowel me but sitting at the table with a glass of water, already sobbing gently. The rage I could have begun to cope with; this, I'm already lost.

"Jenny?"

"What?"

But I don't know what else to say. I don't know what I'm supposed to do. I sit at the table opposite her and a few minutes of silence, broken only by her sniffling, follows.

"I can't keep doing this," she says finally.

"Doing what?"

"I can't keep apologising for you."

"I never asked you to apologise for me. In fact, I'd rather you didn't."

"Well someone has to, when you behave like a fucking coked-up movie star diva or something. What the fuck else am I supposed to do? Just shrug my shoulder and say 'oh what's he like?'"

"I don't know, Jenny. I genuinely don't know what you should do. But I do know that things like that would be easier to avoid if you didn't insist on arranging little get-togethers with my fucking parents. Or anyone, for that matter."

Jenny stands and takes her glass over to the sink. "So I'm not supposed to ever socialise with anyone except you?"

"No," I say, "you can socialise with whoever you want. It's just that I most likely won't want to join you."

"*What?* That's ridiculous, Gary."

"Why? Why is that ridiculous?" I'm standing up myself now and moving over to where she's standing. "Knowing what you know about me, why would you expect anything else?"

"I don't know, I just thought, maybe you'd..."

"Change?"

"I suppose so, yeah. Even if it was just a *tiny* bit. Just enough so that maybe we could go out as a couple and meet friends."

"I don't really have any friends. The people we meet from time to time, they're your friends. I've nothing against them, but they aren't my friends. I barely have any contact with Darren, Jimmy and Aimee anymore, and that's fine by me."

I'm about to mention Craig, but I'm not sure whether I should mention what happened with him. I haven't quite processed it myself yet, and I'm not sure what Jenny's thoughts on me interacting with him would be. She's never met him but regards him as some sort of hero for providing the push that helped bring Jenny and me together, but she's also heard enough tales of his behaviour to be, quite reasonably, a little bit afraid of him.

"So, what are you saying, Gary? Are you telling me you never wanna see anyone else? No friends, no family? Just us?"

"Yes! That's exactly what I'm saying. I only go to work because I have to. I understand there's no way around that, but when I'm finished with work I just wanna come home, shut the door, and be with you. I'm not interested in going out with friends. I don't mind us going to see a film or maybe out for dinner, as long as the place isn't too fucking poncey and it's just us. I don't really wanna see my family but I've agreed to do so because I know it's what you want, but I want that to be *strictly* on my terms from now on. I don't wanna see your family either. I've got nothing against them but I want all that to be kept to a minimum, as far as possible. I realise this makes things awkward for you and I'm sorry, and I know that whenever they do see you they probably spend the entire time asking what the fuck you're doing with me, and they're entitled to, and I'm sorry for putting you in that position, but that's the way it has to be. Honestly, Jenny, if I never *had* to see another person except for you for the rest of my life, I really don't think that would be a problem for me at all. In fact I'd welcome that."

"Well, I'm not sure I can live like that, Gary. I mean, I'm a sociable being. I like being with friends."

"I know that, and I'm not asking you not to do that. If you need or want to go out sometimes, that's fine with me. Just... please don't ask or expect me to come with you. I'll stay here and watch a film, read or go to bed, and be waiting when you get home."

"That's not what a fucking relationship is, Gary!" she shouts. "When you're in a relationship, you do things *together*. You go out *together*. You see people *together*. What you're describing is not a partnership. It's... it's having a flatmate. A flatmate that you have sex with. Occasionally."

Jenny sees the look of discomfort in my eyes.

"I'm sorry, I don't mean anything by that. It's just that what you are describing is not what I'm looking for. I knew when we got together that this wouldn't be an entirely conventional relationship, and I was ready for that. But you've got to meet me partway on some things, Gary. Not even halfway, just partway."

"I have, I've made a lot of effort on some things."

She raises her eyebrows at me.

"Okay, well, some degree of effort on some things."

"Well, how about a bit more effort on some issues? Such as having a social life? With other people?"

"I dunno, I've tried, I don't think I can do any better than this, Jenny."

She sighs and gets herself another glass of water from the tap. "Well, then that's gonna be a problem for us, Gary." She looks up at the clock on the wall. "It's late, I need to get to bed. I think maybe you should sleep on the couch tonight, don't you?"

"Erm..."

"What?"

"I'd rather not."

"Well, of course you'd rather not, but under the circumstances, don't you think it's appropriate for you to do so?"

"Well, I see what you mean, and I realise it's sort of customary for that to happen, but... well..."

"Well what, Gary?"

"It's just that, well, I'm used to our bed. Remember when we first moved in, it took me ages to get used to it? I couldn't sleep properly for weeks. It's lived in now. I've got things set up around it just the way I need. Any change from that would cause a lot of disruption. Then I'd probably struggle to readjust to the bed again, assuming I was eventually allowed back in it."

"Gary. Are you really gonna make *me* sleep on the fucking couch?"

"No! I mean, you could just sleep in our room and still be fucked off with me, but if you're insisting we sleep apart, well, you know, that's sort of your idea, so I don't think it's really fair to make me sleep on it when I don't feel it's a necessary sanction."

"You really should sleep on the couch, Gary. Yes, I think we should sleep apart, and I think – oh fuck it. Fine. *I'll* sleep on the fucking couch, then."

Jenny storms to the bedroom and emerges a few moments later in her pyjamas, carrying her pillow and the thin blanket she keeps on top of her side of the duvet. I should offer to let her have the duvet as the living room can get cold but that would cause as much disruption as me sleeping on the couch.

"Erm, night –"

The door to the living room slams shut. I get myself a drink from the kitchen sink and take it through to the bedroom. I undress, placing my shoes under the bed, folding my jeans and shirt neatly together, before placing them in the laundry bin in the corner wrapped inside a plastic bag, to ensure my own clothes and Jenny's don't come into contact. I place my socks and boxer-shorts inside a second plastic bag, which goes inside the first bag. Every Saturday morning, I'll wash my own clothes separately, with Jenny free to wash hers whenever she pleases.

I put on a plain black T-shirt and a new pair of boxer-shorts and walk through to the bathroom. I take an antibacterial wipe out of the cupboard under the sink and wipe down the taps and sink, and throw the wipe into the red bin, which is used only for cleaning products. I run the taps and wipe any residual antibacterial chemicals away using a fresh section of J-cloth. I open the cabinet above the sink and take out a re-sealable plastic bag which contains my toothbrush. Faecal coliforms are commonly found on toothbrushes tested under lab conditions, and the chances of these micro-organisms being found on toothbrushes increase significantly when you share a bathroom with someone. I run my toothbrush under the hot tap for about half a minute then brush my teeth, starting with thirty seconds on the top, then thirty seconds on the bottom, then the same again for the top, and then back again. I rinse my brush, then add another blob of toothpaste, before cleaning my tongue for thirty seconds. I then floss carefully between all teeth before gargling with antiseptic mouthwash.

I turn the shower on while I take off my boxer-shorts and T-shirt, and take three clean towels from the cupboard. I spend the next twenty minutes in the shower. As I'm about to switch off, I decide that, given the stressful events of the evening, I need a little longer in there. So I leave it on, and stay in there for another forty minutes.

After getting out, I towel myself dry, one towel for my head, one for my torso, one for my lower half. When I'm dry I mop up all the water on the floor using the first towel. I put my boxer-shorts and T-shirt back on and take my evening meds out of the cabinet. I wash them down with a plastic cup I also keep in the cabinet for this purpose alone. I take the wet towels through to the linen bin before getting into bed.

Despite the extra room now afforded me by Jenny's absence, I lie, as usual, flat on my back on my side of the bed. I close my eyes and drift quickly off to sleep, but before I nod off I am hit by the thought that this may be the last time I sleep in this bed.

*

I set my alarm for an hour earlier than usual. Luckily, Jenny seems to have slept well enough on the couch, as the living room is still closed when I finish my morning routine. Of course, it's quite likely that she is wide awake, having slept terribly on what is not the most comfortable couch in the world, and is simply avoiding me. If this is the case, then I'm happy with that, as I don't think I could deal either with the awkwardness or the confrontation that would occur if she was up and about. When I leave the flat, exactly one hour earlier than usual, the living room door is still very much closed.

The walk into work is a much quieter one than usual, with only people at the very lowest end of the pay scale usually required to be up at this time of morning; the roads are mostly free of cars but the buses are still full. When I get into town the last thing I feel like doing is interacting with The Knobhead in the coffee shop, but my need for caffeine is even greater than usual, so I grit my teeth and enter, and am not at all surprised to see him already bouncing around the place like he's had a dozen espressos and a line of speed.

"Hey, man, morning! What can I get ya?"

"A large black coffee, please. Can you make it extra strong?"

"Sure thing, man. One of those days, huh?"

"Well, no. Not yet. The day's barely started. But I'm anticipating one."

"Yeah, I hear ya, man,"

I shake my head as The Knobhead turns away and prepares my coffee.

"Oh," I say, a thought suddenly occurring to me, "have you got any of that stuff I had the other day? The guest coffee?"

"Sure thing. Told you it was good stuff, didn't I?"

"Yes," I answer through gritted teeth. Admitting this man-bunned tit-wank could be right about anything isn't easy. "You did."

*

I get to work to find the place empty. A cleaner is at the far end of the office hoovering, but there seems to be no other sign of life. As I reach my office, I'm startled by a loud voice from the kitchenette.

"Gary!"

I turn to see Eddie stepping out with a mug of coffee.

"You're here early," he says, not missing a trick as usual.

"Yeah," I say, "I... erm..."

"You wanted to get ahead of things, right?"

I decide it won't do me any favours to disappoint him, and I have neither the energy nor the inclination to explain my real reason for being there, so I simply nod.

"Great, man. Good hustle, like." He can barely get his last sentence out through the massive yawn that escapes as he talks.

"How long have you been here, Eddie?"

"Oh, quite a while, like."

I look down at his bare feet, and notice how crumpled his shirt and ankle-length shorts are. "Eddie, have you actually been home?"

"Oh, well, ya know..." He looks embarrassed, like a teenager caught wanking.

"Have you been here all night?"

"Weell, yeah. I mean, I just need to, ya know, get ahead of things too. I mean, it's a bit of an intense time here. What with, well..."

"Phil?" I say quietly, just in case he's here.

"Yeah, Phil," Eddie answers sadly. "Gaz, you're an honest guy, you always tell it like it is. What's your take on him? Phil, I mean."

"He's a resounding cunt, Eddie. He's part spin doctor, part motivational speaker, part assassin. But *all* cunt."

Eddie lets out a bashful little laugh, as though he's never heard anyone swear before. "Yeah," he says, "he is a bit of a cunt, isn't he?"

I sense an opportunity here to try and gain an ally in my fight for survival. Eddie is the one person here who thinks I'm anything other than a weirdo or an imposter.

"Eddie, why is he *really* here?"

"Well, he got sent down from head—"

"No, I know why he's here. What I mean is, can't you do something about it? Can't you... I mean, he's just gonna ruin what's so... unique about this place." I hope that appealing to Eddie's vanity, his sense of pride might help, as might dropping in a few of the ridiculous phrases he likes to use. "I mean, he's just gonna ruin the vibe here. There's such an... energy about this place, and he just doesn't get it, you know? He's just not one of us, Eddie. *He's not CUltureSHock people.*"

Eddie is nodding along with me, and seems somewhere between tears and a rousing outburst. "You're right, Gaz. You're *so* right, man." I feel my spirits lift. "But there's nothing I can do." And I feel my spirits sink again. "I'm not the boss anymore. Not really. I mean, I'm still the boss here, but I sold up, man. I sold out. I wish I hadn't now, but they offered so much money, and they were willing to pay me more than I was even paying myself. I couldn't refuse. But I know now it was a mistake. We tried to run before we could walk. We were like that guy that flew too close to the sun."

"Icarus?"

"No, the guy that flew too close to the sun."

"That was Icarus."

"You sure?"

"I'm pretty certain, yeah."

He shakes his head in wonder. "See, Gaz. That's part of why I wanted you here. You've got that unique perspective. That knowledge and experience."

Again, I see no need to disillusion him or point out that employing someone like me is a perfect example of the poor judgement that has led him into this situation.

"Anyway," he says, looking at his watch, "best get to it. Phil will be here any minute. He's always in early. That's why I started coming in early. He kept making remarks about me being late in and stuff. Wouldn't be surprised if he ends up getting rid of me."

"He wouldn't do that, would he?"

"I dunno, he doesn't seem to like me very much."

"I know the feeling."

"Have a good day, Gaz."

"You too, Eddie."

*

I get to my desk and pop a couple of Amitriptyline before I even sit down. Given the circumstances, I feel I'm likely to need more of a boost than usual. As my computer fires up, I hear a flurry of activity from the main office. Crouching down slightly behind my computer I see Phil in a pair of tight lycra cycling shorts, fluorescent vest over a sleeveless T-shirt that reveals his bulging biceps, stomping through the office like Paul Bunyan. As he turns towards my office, I see that the only thing bulging more than his biceps is the vast, swinging schlong that is flopping about, Lynford Christie style, in his cycling shorts. It's a disgusting sight, like a Cumberland sausage thrown into a tombola. But, like many things one would rather not see, having set eyes on it, I'm powerless to look away. As it approaches me, I'm able to drag my eyes away from it long enough to register that Phil has been watching me watching him. Or watching me watching his genitals.

Having registered my presence, he changes direction to head straight towards my office. As he barges in, I jump into my chair and start clicking away at my keyboard. He appears in his usual position to the left of me, and probably notices before I do that my computer screen isn't even on yet. Despite the futility of it, I continue typing away.

"Morning, Gary. In early today, I see. Great stuff."

"Yeah, just... catching up on a few things," I say, looking at the black screen. I finally give up this particular charade and turn towards Phil. Or, more accurately, towards the cock that is dangling centimetres above my desk and less than a foot away from my face. I move my eyes upwards to Phil's, and see that he's looking at my computer screen, highlighting just how pathetic my behaviour has been.

"And would any of those things be the report? Time's getting on, Gary. I feel like I've been patient up to now."

"Yes, I'm hoping to make a start on it today, I've just got a few things I need to... erm... action first. I mean, you wouldn't want me to neglect my official duties, would you?"

"Well, no. I suppose not. Let's not leave it too much longer, though, yeah?"

"Yeah. I mean no. I mean, yeah, I won't."

My eyes move back down, being drawn once again to his knob, then back to my screen, which has finally fired up. I log in and try to look busy. After a brief pause, Phil leaves my office. I watch him head straight into the kitchenette and take his fucking yoghurt shite out of the fridge and take a big spoonful of it whilst leaning casually against the sideboard, which causes his dick to jut out even further.

*

I grind my way through the morning, sending and scheduling tweets, tracking trends and trying to insert CUltureSHock into them in some way, when I get a Twitter notification of a new follower. I click on the icon to see who it is.

@BuckleProductions followed you, it says.

I make sure nobody is watching me and click on the profile. The avatar is of a young woman wearing nothing but a pair of knee-high leather boots, sticking both her middle fingers up and grimacing at the camera. Her right leg is raised slightly, and underneath the spiked heel of the boot is a middle-aged man in a suit and tie, lying prone on the floor. There's something about the woman that is eerily familiar. She looks too young to be someone I would have seen back in my days of actually watching pornography, but I can't place her. I'm amazed to see that the account has a blue verification tick and over two hundred thousand followers, while it follows less than a hundred. Clearly Craig has made more of a success of the online smut business than I had given him credit for.

I consider blocking the account, wary of allowing pornographic accounts like this to follow the official company one, but I take my lunch out of my bag and eat it while I scroll through the tweets. Most of them are simply links to short clips of their own videos. I finish my lunch and lean back in my chair, still trying to place the woman's face. I reach into my desk, and take two Diazepam tablets. I check my phone to see if there's been any communication from Jenny, but am not remotely surprised to see that there hasn't. I grab my jacket and head out of the door.

*

After my first visit to what seems to be the UK's most successful hard-core porn enterprise, I had wandered back to CUltureSHock in something of a daze, so it takes me a while to figure out where Craig's studio is. I'd ask for directions but I can't imagine that asking a stranger where the local filth studio is would go over too well. Plus, I'd have to talk to a stranger.

Eventually I find a familiar looking back alley somewhere off Dale Street, and a building with an intercom, most of the buttons to which are unallocated except for a security firm and Buckle Productions. It occurs to me that each of these could belong to Craig as I hesitantly push the button for the one I know is his, having pulled my sleeve down over my finger.

"BUCKLE!!"

"Erm, Craig, it's me. Gary. Gary Lennon."

There's a short pause.

"I know who it is, you weird fucking cunt. Come up."

He buzzes me in and I climb the couple of flights of steps. Opening the door tentatively, I detect an odd odour that I can't quite place, and hear Craig's voice from the far side.

"Over here, Gaz."

I follow the sound of his voice to find him sat at his desk wearing just a pair of tracksuit bottoms.

"Alright, Gaz," he says without looking away from his screen.

"How did you know it was me?"

"Who the fuck else would it be? I don't get unexpected visitors."

"So I was expected?"

He stops whatever he's doing on his computer and looks up at me, nodding as though I've asked a ridiculous question.

"Why?" I ask.

"How could you not come back after last time? Strange as it was, I think it intrigued you."

"Intrigued me?"

"Yeah, I think you wanna know about what I'm doing here."

"What, making porn?"

"No, that's not all I do here, although it's a shame you weren't here half an hour ago, you'd have caught the tail end of another shoot."

"So that's what that smell is," I say, retching slightly.

"Yup, the smell of Buckle juice."

"Fucking hell, Craig."

"Oh, I'm sorry, Gaz. You're absolutely right, mate. I should stop earning a living on the off-chance you might pop over, eh?"

"No, of course not. Where are your... er..."

"Co-stars?"

"Yeah, I suppose so."

"They've gone out for a bit, we're alone for now."

"Okay. So, when you say 'what you're doing here', what do you actually mean?"

He smiles at me and beckons me close to his desk. He turns the screen towards me to reveal many windows of various websites, some windows of coding that I don't even begin to comprehend.

"What is this?"

"All these websites," he says, pointing towards the windows onscreen, "belong to various far-right groups, some pro-ISIS groups, Christian fundamentalist groups, shit like that."

"Right."

"And this coding here, this is what helps me hack into these fuckers, and carry out a little website renovation for them."

"Renovation?"

"Oh yes. This group of fucking backwards, cave-dwelling, jihadi-loving shitwits here? Whenever one of their brainwashed, unfulfilled, KFC-working followers clicks on their site, the first thing they'll see is a clip of the most hard-core gay porn I could find. These fire-and-brimstone, funeral-disrupting, inbred, American South fucknuts? Follow any link to their homepage, and you'll see a looping clip of yours truly unloading a heroically large, five-day load of jizz directly into the camera. The neo-Nazi, alt-right scum get a clip of a beautiful, blonde haired white girl getting gangbanged by a bunch of home-boys with cocks the size of fire extinguishers. And, as a nice little extra, the second any of them try to remove anything I've added, they get hit with a particularly nasty virus I created. So their websites are fucked, and their PCs and laptops get struck down with a virulent bout of electronic Ebola."

I can't help but smile.

"I know you have to spend all day online, Gaz, and I know you must come across these fucking shit sprinklers. You know who I mean, fucking micro-cocked dweebs who just a few years ago were getting their heads dunked in shit- and piss-filled school bogs and having their pale, bare arses whipped with towels by people like me. Now they've got a fucking internet connection and a cheap webcam, they spend their time in their fat mother's spare room recording fucking hate-filled diatribes, which they then post on their social media and websites for the *even more* pathetic friendless little virgins that make up their following to fucking lap up without the slightest fucking question as to whether they're actually fucking correct. Then there's the fucking men's rights movement. I mean, fucking men's rights? Do I need to say any more about *that* fucking crowd, Gaz? There's fucking Brexiters, there's fucking nasty little anonymous trolls who seem to think that telling some poor random bod that their disabled kid should be put down will give their fucking lives meaning. And, unfuckingsurprisingly, these cunts all seem to overlap. They all seem to share the same fucking negative, self-and-everyone-else-loathing world view. Then there's these fucking jihadi wannabe gangster pretenders who 'like' reports of ISIS attacks in Europe and spout shit about it being the will of Allah, without ever having the guts to show their faces or blow their own fucking stupid selves up."

I realise I've been nodding along with every single point of Craig's speech, and even that my mouth is hanging open. I regain some composure.

"Yes, Okay. I've seen these people. And yes, it drives me fucking mental. I fucking hate them, all of them, as much as you do. But why do you think I'm intrigued by it, and why are you so keen for me to see this?"

He rubs his hands together, gets up from his desk and gets a can from the fridge. I decline his offer of one while he walks around his studio.

"I need your help, Gaz. Well, I *want* your help."

"With what?"

"My work. And no, not the porn. You'd be shit at that, you fucking prude."

149

"My help? It looks like you've got it covered, and seem to be having fun."

"It's not about fun, Gaz. It's about more than that. It's about starting a movement. It's about striking back at these nasty fucks before they take over."

"Whoa, what the fuck are you on about, Craig? This sounds like you're about to branch into some sort of fucking urban terrorist shite or something like that."

He holds his hands up as I'm talking. "No, it's not like that. Well, okay, it *is* like that. Kind of. But not really. Look, just trust me... nobody will get hurt. Not physically, anyway."

"How, then?"

Before he can answer, the studio door opens and two women walk in. The first is a tall blonde, the second one I recognise from the avatar I was looking at earlier. I still can't place her, but as she looks over at me she squints as though thinking the exact same thing. The blonde one barely even registers I'm there.

"Ah, Gary, these are my colleagues," Craig says, beckoning them over. "Gary, this is Anna." He gestures towards the blonde.

"Hello," she says in an Eastern European accent.

"And this," Craig says, putting his arm round the other one's waist, "this is Lorna. You remember Lorna, don't you? Lorna, you remember Gary?"

Again, we squint at each other, but both shake our heads.

"Gary," he says to Lorna, taking a swig from his can, "is the fella whose flat I took you back to that first time we met by Birkenhead Park."

Suddenly it all comes back to me. During Craig's last re-entry into my life, having installed himself in my flat whilst on the run, having ripped off a bouncer's nose and gone AWOL from the army, I was awoken one night by Craig, who, in a warped gesture that in his world would have seemed generous and loving, had hired a prostitute to help address what he considered to be my sexual repression. I quite rudely told him to get her out of my flat, and now she is standing in front of me, her expression changing from one of confused interest to one of disgust and anger.

"Oh, so THAT'S where I recognise you from. You're that fucking stuck-up little prick who thought he was too good to fuck me, eh? I fucking remember now."

"No, it wasn't a case of being too good, I just didn't want to. It wasn't anything personal."

"What is this?" Anna has now wandered back over to the group, her attention clearly having been caught by the raised voices.

"This is the little twat I told you about. The one who wouldn't fuck me that night I met Buckle."

"Ah, I have heard this story," Anna says, moving round to the front of me and inspecting me up and down. "Hmm," she says. "From look of him, I would say he is homosexual. Or impotent. Or impotent homosexual. With small cock."

Craig is laughing along with this description. "Fucking hell, she's got you on all counts there, mate."

"Fuck off!" I shout at him. I turn back to Anna. "No, I'm not homosexual, or impotent. I just didn't want to have sex with her. I just told her, it wasn't personal. It just... wasn't the right circumstances."

"Hmm." She inspects me some more. "Maybe not homo, but you carry yourself like a man with a very small penis. All hunched up, no confidence in your movement."

"It's nothing to do with that, I'm just... I'm just not very confident. It's fuck all to do with having a small penis. I mean, I haven't got a small penis."

"Take it out," Anna demands.

"*What?*"

"Take out your penis, show it to me. Let me see if it is small."

"No fucking way, why would I do that?"

"Little cock!" Lorna shouts. I look imploringly at Craig, who is holding his hand over his mouth but shaking with laughter.

"Oh, fuck this shit," I say. "Why am I standing here being demeaned and insulted by a fucking porn star and a prozzie?"

I storm towards the door.

"Bye-bye, little dick man," Anna shouts after me.

"Twat!" Lorna yells.

I slam the door shut but Craig catches up with me before I reach the top of the stairs. "Sorry about that, Gaz," he says, still laughing.

"Fuck off, Craig."

"Oh, don't be like that. And don't worry about them. Anna's always like that. She's very forthright in her views, like. And Lorna, well, you'd probably just hurt her feelings. You should apologise, really."

"Fucking apologise?"

"Hahaha, just messing. Listen, Gaz, never mind what went on in there. I'm serious about what I was talking about before. I want you on board, Gaz. I think you need this, too."

"Why would I need this? What could I possibly have to gain?"

"Look, I know you're not happy, mate. It's obvious. I mean, even by your standards. You need something, mate. You need some fucking action in your life. An outlet. Just listen to what I've got planned, man. You'll wanna be involved, I'm sure of it. Just come back inside, I'll sort things out with the girls. Just come and listen to what I've got going on." He opens the door to the studio and nods his head towards it. "You coming or not, Gaz?"

"Fuck off, Craig," I say and head down the stairs. When I get to the bottom I look up and see him peering over the hand-rails at me.

"You'll be back, my mate. And when you do come back, you'll be welcome."

"Don't contact me again," I shout up. "Don't call me, don't research me and definitely don't fucking kidnap me. *Unfollow* me. In every sense."

*

There's a meeting going on in Eddie's office when I get back. Or rather Phil is having a meeting with Eddie, in Eddie's office. From what I can see, Phil is the only one really doing any talking, while Eddie sits on one of the bean bags on the floor, looking like a reception school child being admonished by his teacher. They see me looking in and I lock eyes with Phil for a split second. He walks towards me and I turn and head towards my own office, but he catches up with me before I get there.

"Hi, Gary," he says.

"Hi Phil, Just heading back to—"

"To your *office*, yes," he interrupts, with that strange emphasis on the word "office". "I notice that, apart from Eddie, the boss, you're actually the only person here with their own private office, yeah?"

"Erm, that's right."

"Interesting, really. I mean, it just kind of gets me wondering exactly why that is. I mean, I'm not saying you don't need or deserve it, I'm just curious really."

"Well, I..."

"That's okay, I don't expect you to explain it to me right here and now. You can just put it in your evaluation. Maybe explain why you think it is that you're afforded that particular privilege. And one or two others."

"Others?"

"Well, I hear that you have an arrangement that, although they're allowed to hoover in there, the cleaners aren't allowed to touch your desk or anything on it. Is that right too?"

"Well, yes, but..."

He holds his hand up to stop me, his face full of smug affability, with an undercurrent of menace. "Gary, it's fine. Just put it in the evaluation."

And he walks back to Eddie's office, where Eddie, halfway up from his bean bag, hovers awkwardly for a moment before sitting back down.

"Fucking twat," I mutter, heading towards my office. "Fucking smug, suave fucking cunt."

I pass the kitchenette. And stop by the door.

I have an idea.

I instantly dismiss it as stupid and ridiculous, and carry on walking. Three steps later, I stop again. It is a ridiculous idea. Childish. Pointless. But I can't step any further. I look around and see that nobody is watching me or looking in my direction. I step back and into the kitchenette, and open the fridge door. What I'm looking for is straight ahead of me on a shelf all on its own as though it was waiting for me. I take out Phil's yoghurt and take another discreet look around. I take the lid off and look at the weird, gloopy shite in there. I take one last scan around and summon up a thick wad of spit, which I gob straight into the pot. I put the lid back on and give it a little shake to mix it in, place it back in the fridge and leave.

Returning to my own office, though, I feel like I've missed an opportunity. Without any further hesitation, I stride back into the kitchenette. A quick look around reassures me the coast is still clear.

I grab the yoghurt pot and take it to the toilets near to my office and lock myself in a cubicle. My heart is pounding now and I'm virtually hyperventilating. I place the pot on the cistern and take my cock out and begin masturbating. Unfortunately, and not surprisingly given my inability to be remotely sexually spontaneous, my cock doesn't respond. It's like trying to milk an empty cow through an entirely flaccid udder. I close my eyes and think about tits, arses, vaginas, but nothing seems to work. I concentrate harder and think about *Jenny's* tits, *Jenny's* arse, *Jenny's* vagina, and it starts to work. I'm instantly semi-hard, and can feel my balls tightening. I think about the first time I had sex with Jenny, her beautiful naked body against mine, the look in her eyes as she pulled me inside her, and now I'm hard, I wank harder and faster and as I'm about to come I realise I've forgotten the whole purpose of this act and grab the pot just in time to shoot a few thick arcs of jizz right into it. It lands in the gloopy yoghurt with a heavy *plop* and I squeeze every last drop before I close the lid, shaking it around again to mix it all in. I remove the lid to make sure it's sufficiently mixed in before I clean myself up and sneak the pot back into the fridge.

I sit back at my desk, aware that the act I have just committed was disgusting, juvenile and possibly criminal. But for the next few hours I find myself smiling for the first time in a long time.

SEVENTEEN

The smile subsides as the afternoon moves on. As I get towards leaving time it has turned into a full-blown frown as I contemplate what to do. I don't know whether I'll be welcome back at the flat, and even if I am I don't know if I can deal with the anxiety of going back there and churning up what happened last night with Jenny. By the end of my working day, I'm sitting at my desk almost in tears, paralysed by fear and indecision.

I won't be able to stay much longer without drawing attention to myself, so eventually I leave the office and begin walking vaguely in the direction of home, but find myself taking several detours, often circling back on myself. After nearly half an hour of this, I decide to go into The Vernon Arms, and order myself a Guinness. Thankfully, the pub is almost empty, so I'm able to sit in peace and drink my pint while I try to figure out my course of action.

Before I've finished my first pint I'm back at the bar, draining the dregs as the barman pulls me another pint and a double whiskey. I knock the whiskey back and order another as the second Guinness settles. I take the second pint and a third double whiskey back to my corner table, and a horrid lucidity hits me.

YOU CAN NEVER GO HOME AGAIN.

I down the second pint as quickly as I down the third double shot, and stagger out of the pub and find myself staggering, without conscious decision, towards Moorfields train station. I buy a can of the strongest lager I can find from the Spar before I head into the station and buy a ticket.

I've missed the worst of the rush-hour commuters but the platform is busy enough to put me straight onto the verge of a panic attack. I reach into my pocket and take two Diazepam from the box that I took out of my desk before leaving and knock them back with a big swig of the disgusting lager. I clamber onto the first train to Birkenhead and lean against the door as it closes. I stare at my reflection in the glass of the door opposite me as we head into the tunnel. My eyes are wild with the mix of alcohol, Diazepam and anxiety.

Arriving at Hamilton Square station I walk up the steps to the lift, and everyone around me backs into the corner furthest away from the weird-looking bloke with frenzy in his eyes and shit lager in his hand. I walk out of the station onto the street and round to Hamilton Square itself. I finish the last of the can and fling it over the knee-high fence, and a passing woman tuts at me. I walk round to Market Street and do a quick eeny-meeny-miny-moe between Hornblowers and The Lion. The Lion wins. The woman behind the bar eyes me suspiciously as I order a Guinness, but decides to serve me.

"Actually," I say, before she's started pulling it, "I'll have a pint of Carling and a bottle of Blue WKD."

When in Rome.

She looks at me as though I'm taking the piss, but then shrugs her shoulders and opens the WKD, which I finish before the Carling has been pulled.

"And a double vodka," I say as she places the pint down.

I pay and take the drinks to a nearby table as my phone begins to vibrate in my pocket. It's a message from Jenny.

- *You're not home?* it says. I stare at my phone for a few minutes, unsure of how to respond, if at all. I take a gulp of the pissy, watery lager and text back.

- *In Birko.* I respond.

- *Why???* comes the almost immediate reply.

- *Not sure.*

- *Are you OK?*

- *Don't know. It's all a bit of a mess isn't it?*

- *Gary, do I need to be worried here?*

- *More than usual?*

- *I'm serious, Gary!!*

- *I'm not going to do anything fatal.*

- *Are you going to your mum's?*

That thought genuinely hadn't even occurred to me. I didn't even consciously plan to come to Birkenhead or to end up sitting in a pub already pissed at barely seven o'clock. I don't think I'm likely to go anywhere near my parent's house, but decide that letting Jenny believe I am is probably the best option.

- *Think so.*

- *Staying over?*

- *Will see how it goes.*

- *OK. Speak soon.*

- *Bye.*

I finish my drinks and leave, heading straight into the nearby offie. I ask the man behind the counter for a packet of twenty Regal.

"No, make it twenty Benson and Hedges, please."

As he slides one door shut and opens the other, I change my mind again.

"Wait! Make it twenty Lambert and Butler."

The newsagent gives me an *"are you taking the piss?"* look, but reopens the first door and throws the ciggies onto the counter. I pay for them, and a disposable lighter. I rip the packet open, throwing the thin plastic cover on the floor of the shop, and light one up before I'm even out of the door. As I step outside, I take a huge drag on it. I haven't smoked in almost a year, and the rush of nicotine, combined with the booze, almost knocks me over. I take another drag, even deeper than the first. I suck the little death stick so hard I can taste the fucking cancer. I finish it on the third drag and instantly light another as I walk the few doors down to Hornblowers. I order more shitty lager, a luminous yellow alcopop I've never heard of before and a double Malibu, simply because it's in my eye line.

"Wanna buy some bacon, lad?"

I turn towards the voice and see a dishevelled man who could be aged anywhere between twenty and forty, but it's impossible to tell with his sallow complexion, sunken eyes and pockmarked skin.

"What?"

"Wanna buy some bacon?"

"Are you a butcher?" I say.

"Yer wha'?"

"Are you a butcher? You're selling bacon, so I wondered if you're a butcher."

"Do I look like a fucking butcher?"

I look him up and down, his tatty old tracksuit, his trainers almost falling apart. No butcher's pinny to be seen.

"Not really. But you could be off duty," I say.

"Look, do you wanna buy some fucking bacon or not, ya prick?"

"Oi!"

We both turn to see the landlord standing by a door leading out to the bar.

"Fuck off out of it, you!"

For a minute, I'm not sure whether he's talking to me or the pork salesman, but it's the latter that responds to the order first.

"Fucking nice one, ya twat," he says as he storms out of the pub. I finish my odd collection of drinks and head into the toilets to empty my bladder before staggering back to the bar and ordering another random assortment of drinks, my choices drawing puzzled looks from the barman and other drinkers.

After another round, it's now nine o'clock and I'm barely able to maintain verticality. I sense that I'm unlikely to be served any more drinks, so I wobble out into the cool Birkenhead air. I walk round to Conway Street and stop outside Sherlock's nightclub. As I reach the door a bouncer plants a meaty hand on my chest.

"Sorry, mate," he says.

"What for?"

"You're not coming in. Not in that state."

"I'm not that pissed," I say, not really looking at him, hoping that if he can't see my eyes he won't be able to tell how pissed I am.

"You're fucking pissed enough. You should be coming out of here in that state, not going in. Go 'ead. Off home, mate."

I look up at him now and focus my eyes on his. "You can never go home again," I say.

"Well I don't give a fuck where you go, but you're not coming in here, now do one."

I decide any further protest is pointless and carry on down Conway Street. A few doors down is a new establishment. "Peachez Gentleman's Club". It seems Birkenhead now has its very own lap dancing club. As I approach it, a bouncer, who has no doubt just witnessed my unsuccessful attempt to gain ingress to Sherlock's, is watching me.

"Don't even think about it," he says firmly as I reach him. I simply lift a hand and carry on walking, deciding that telling him I'd have no desire whatsoever to have some Birko scrag-end thrusting her vagina in my face would only put my physical safety at risk. Walking through the bus station, I wonder if, given that it's now ten o'clock and even some of Birkenhead's worst locations are now refusing me entry, I should think about going home. But then I think of a place that will have no qualms about letting in even someone in my inebriated state. A place without such exacting standards. A place where nobody knows your name, and nobody gives a fuck what it is. I pick up my pace and walk past the Asda, round the corner, across the road and into Moodz bar. On one of the four corners of hell, only

Moodz and McDonald's now remain, The Charing Cross and the ever-changing bar on the other corners now having finally closed their doors for good. The dream is over for them, but in Moodz, the nightmare is in full swing. As soon as I enter, I trip over something and land face first on the floor.

"Watch where you're fucking going, lad," I hear from behind me. I look round and realise I've tripped over a mobility scooter, the occupant of which is looking down at me, a huge gut spilling out from under his shirt, fading tattoos covering his arms.

"Sorry," I mutter, and carry on towards the bar as I feel his glare burning into my back. I take a spot at the bar vacated by two old fellas who look like they could be related to the bloke who tried to sell me bacon earlier. I order myself a bottle of Budweiser and a Smirnoff Ice. I'm getting a few looks from the punters but at this point I'm unsure whether they're threatening looks or just looks of curiosity. I'm the youngest person in here by at least fifteen years, I'm wearing my work clothes and, by comparison, I'm very clean cut. Most of the Moodz clientele appear to have lived lives of toil and pain, their eyes appear to have seen things I wouldn't believe. Their skin is leathery, scarred and discoloured. The men are even worse. As I knock my rank, chemical-filled drinks back, everyone seems to gradually lose interest in me, so I sit at the vacant bar stool and order some more.

The hours of solid boozing on an empty stomach finally begin to catch up with me and I feel my eyelids beginning to droop. I'm dragged out of my stupor, however, by a chorus of cheers and a loud yell of "turn it up, mate" from beside me. I realise that the "it" in question is Queen's "Don't Stop Me Now" and the Moodz clientele fucking love it. The sound is turned up full blast, filling the bar, and the place comes to horrible, disturbing life.

The bloke on the mobility scooter has his shirt off and is swinging it round his head, driving his scooter up and down as much in time to the music as a mobility scooter can go, a friend standing on the back of it, punching the air and singing along at the top of his voice. The entire bar becomes an impromptu dance floor as couples and singles alike dance, jump and sing along to one of the shittest songs of all time, by one of the shittest bands of all time.

From in amongst the throng of dancers, a figure emerges. A woman dances her way towards me, her dance moves clearly aimed in my direction. She's pushing fifty, wearing a white vest top, her chunky arms on display, a faded tattoo on her left bicep. A bra strap hangs down over the top of the opposite arm. Her denim mini-skirt exposes pale, blotchy legs, a deep bruise visible above her left knee. If someone who had never been to or heard of Birkenhead asked for a visual representation of the town, this woman wouldn't be a bad shout. She may have been quite attractive at one time but, like a Birko Blanche Dubois, her life experiences have drained whatever beauty there may have been, leaving only the kind of sunken eyes so many in this town see through. She dances closer towards me clumsily on her heels.

"Alright, love," she shouts over Brian May's distinctively muted guitar squealings.

"Hello," I slur.

"What's yer name?"

"Ruddiger," I lie, not knowing why.

"Hiya Rodney, I'm Tracey," she says.

"Of course you are."

"Not seen you in here before."

"Never ventured in before."

"Well I'm glad you did," Tracey says flirtatiously. "We don't normally get smart, good looking young lads like you in here."

She lifts her arms above her head and spins around, clearly wanting me to give a full appraisal of the goods currently on offer. I'm not sure whether it's this sight or the accumulated lager, spirits and Day-Glo alcopops inside me, but I feel slightly queasy.

"Nah, they're all in Sherlock's," I say.

"Then why aren't *you* in there?"

"They wouldn't let me in," I say, my feelings only now hurt by this fact.

"Stuck up fuckers," Tracey says, offended on my behalf. "I'd *let you in* any time." She winks at me, as though this last line was too subtle for me, and I feel a lot queasier.

"That's most hospitable of you," I say, unable to think of any other response. Tracey leans in closer, her hand now over my shoulder.

"Tell you what, Rodney. I only live round the corner. Why don't we go back to mine and I'll show you just how much I'd like to let you in."

She leans back, her eyes fixed "seductively" on mine. I give her my best attempt at a sexy grin, and motion for her to lean back in with my finger. She places her ear next to my mouth.

"Tracey," I say, "I'd rather suck a dead tramp's dick than put my own dick anywhere near your saggy, over-used, stinking fucking Birkenhead cider-minge."

She leans back, aghast, now, quite contrary to the sentiments of the song that's still playing, clearly not having such a good time, and the look of shock on her face quickly turns to one of rage. She swings a punch at me that connects somewhere in the middle of my throat, knocking me off the bar stool.

"Fucking little cunt!" she yells at me.

Even over the sound of the music, our altercation has been heard, and people are turning to look at us, and I quickly assess the mood as one of protectiveness of a regular patron, coupled with the already established suspicion of the unknown interloper instantly moving up several notches. I'm certain I hear a male patron growl, and possibly a hoof being scraped angrily on the floor. I think about offering each of them one of my L&B as a peace offering, but decide the only way to avoid a lynching is to make a run for it, so I bolt towards the door. As I do, Tracey delivers an impressive punch to the back of my neck, which knocks me off balance. Before I reach the door, the bloke on the mobility scooter drives towards me at full speed in an attempt to run me over. I attempt to side-step him, but he catches me on the back of the leg, knocking me further off balance. I change direction involuntarily and am now heading towards the large glass window that makes up the facade of Moodz.

I try to right myself but a further shove from an unknown party sends me crashing through the window and out onto the street. I land on my back with a heavy thud amongst the shattered glass, as the sound of Freddie Mercury's voice fills the air. I quickly check to see if I've cut any major arteries or vessels. There's no major blood spillage but I can tell without even looking that there's some glass in my face. I stand up and I think it's only the shock of seeing the shards of glass sticking out of me, probably giving me the appearance of a cut-price version of Pinhead from *Hellraiser*, that stops the Moodz clientele giving me a further kicking.

I stagger into the road and hear a car screech as it swerves to avoid me and crashes into a wall or barrier somewhere behind me. I reach the other side of the road, where the handful of people inside McDonald's have gathered at the window to watch the events unfold. I lock eyes with one customer, a bloke standing with his daughter. He looks me up and down and silently mouths 'Are you okay?' I nod, then projectile vomit all over the window. Multi-coloured drinks spray out of me, leaving a horrible rainbow running down the glass between us. The bloke inside, upon seeing it, instantly vomits his own fast food all over the other side of it. In response, his daughter then vomits all over the sleeve of his jacket. I want to reassure him that this is far from the most disgusting vomit-related incident in my life, and to apologise for having probably ruined his only court-sanctioned night of visitation with his daughter, but manage only to shout sorry as I stagger away.

My now empty stomach growls, and I wish I'd bought that bacon earlier. As I stagger away, another punch, possibly from someone inside Moodz, someone inside McDonald's, or most likely the driver of the car, connects with the side of my head, knocking me to the ground. I curl into a ball and wait for the kicks and punches to follow, but am relieved that only a yell of "Fucking stupid twat!" and a single kick to the base of my spine follow.

I pick myself up and carry on down towards the bus station. My back twisted from the painful kick, my body aches all over from the accumulative pounding I've just taken, causing me to shuffle along like a Birkenheadian Richard III. Before I reach the bus station I get to a public toilet outside the market. It's one of those black, Tardis-like, standalone ones with the sliding doors that open when you put twenty pence in. I get inside, close the door and assess my injuries in the mirror above the sink. There's about a dozen shards of varying size sticking out of my face, the smallest about the size of a pea, the largest about the size of one of the chicken nuggets the unfortunate fella in McDonald's had vomited all over his arm by his daughter. I pick them out as carefully as a man as pissed as I am can manage, dropping the bits into the sink. I splash water all over my face. The cuts aren't deep, but they are bleeding. In the absence of anything else, I tear off some sheets of toilet paper and stick them against the wounds, as one would with shaving cuts. The blood trickling from the wounds keeps the pieces of tissue in place and I decide there's little else I can do, so I leave the toilet and continue my aimless trek down Conway Street. I turn the corner onto Argyle Street and am drawn, like a moth to the flames, into Capone's takeaway. After assuring the man behind the counter that I'm fine, I order the largest doner kebab available, a large portion of cheesy chips, a meat feast pizza and two cans of Irn-Bru to wash it all down.

"Smells fucking delicious, that," I say as I hand over the last note in my wallet and carry my food towards Hamilton Square. I sit on a bench and eat my food, chilli and garlic sauce, cheese and grease covering my hands and face, but right now I don't care. I just hope it doesn't seep into my cuts and cause an infection. Which, judging by the stinging, it probably is doing.

After I finish my food I fling the boxes and cartons behind my head and lean back on the bench, exhausted. I wonder if I can sink any lower than this evening before I realise that the evening isn't over yet. I'm in Birkenhead, the trains are finished and I now have no energy to find a taxi, and probably couldn't speak coherently enough to direct one to Aigburth even if I did. In any event, I couldn't possibly turn up home in this state. There's no way I'm going to my mum and dad's, so there's only one thing for it. I step over the low fence and walk across the grass, find the thickest bush, and push my way into the middle of it. After using the light from my phone to ensure no homeless people have either set up home, died or shat

in there, I lie down on the ground, pull my coat around myself and go to sleep.

EIGHTEEN

I awake from a dream in which I'm drowning in Blue WKD to the sound of early morning commuters on their way to early shifts or on their way home from late shifts. Turning towards the path I see that my temporary resting place, thick and leafy as it seemed in darkness, is clearly visible in daylight, and I'm drawing strange looks from passers-by. Thanks to the best part of a decade of Tory austerity, the sight of large numbers of homeless people is now an entirely everyday and mundane one around Birkenhead and Liverpool city centre, as it is in most towns and cities in Britain, so the sight of one here, a location frequented by those with no other choice, isn't unusual in itself. What is unusual is the sight of their ranks being joined by a man in smart office clothes, with toilet paper stuck to parts of his face with dried blood.

I reach for my phone and there is just sufficient battery power for it to tell me that the time is 7:43 a.m., so as well as everything else, I'm also now on course to be late for work. I struggle to my feet and the true force of my hangover hits me. My head is banging, my ears ringing, and I nearly keel straight over. All I can taste is something resembling blood, probably a combination of the mystery meat kebab and the actual blood that has presumably been trickling down into my mouth from one of the many wounds, external or internal.

I check my pockets. My wallet is still there, all cards too, showing that I was, surprisingly, not mugged whilst comatose on the ground. A quick audit of my trousers tells me they haven't been tampered with, which, coupled with the lack of anal discomfort, reassures me that I have also not been raped, a discovery which is likely to be the highpoint of my day.

I gather my bearings and walk towards the train station. My throat is so dry I can barely speak to purchase a ticket, so I buy a bottle of water and a packet of paracetamol before I take the lift down to the platform. Most people give me a wide berth as I get onto the train, so I'm able to secure a row of seats to myself. I wouldn't usually allow my arse to come into contact with the tattered fabric of a Merseyrail seat for fear that some form of bacteria would be transferred onto my clothing, then through it and up into my anus, where it would then grow, multiply and consume me from within, but the way I feel right now, I'd welcome any such occurrence. As I leave the train and take the escalator down onto Moorfields, I receive another message from Jenny.

- *Where are you? Are you OK? What happened?*

I can't even begin to outline the events of last night in a text, plus my phone only has five percent battery power remaining, so I simply reply *"Just getting into work"*, knowing that'll buy me the rest of the day to come up with something.

As I enter CUltureSHock, any hopes I had of avoiding people, especially my key antagonist, are dashed instantly by the sight of Phil and Eddie standing at the top of the stairs, deep in conversation. They turn to nod good morning at me, but both instantly do a double-take.

"Christ almighty, Gary," Phil says, looking me up and down. "What the fuck happened to you?"

"Erm, bit of a rough night," I croak.

"A rough night? Gary, you've got bits of tissue and dried blood all over your face. And you look like you slept in a hedge."

"Funny you should say that..."

Phil asks Eddie to leave us alone, which he obligingly does, padding off in his flip-flops. Phil guides me to a quieter corner and moves in closer, then steps back when he gets a hit of my morning shit-breath.

"Look, Gary, all differences aside, what I said the other day about the support that's available, it still stands. I mean, it's clear you've had some sort of relapse –"

"Phil," I interrupt, unable to deal with Phil's paradoxical compassionate-bully-boy tactics right now. "I haven't had a relapse. I've got nothing to relapse into. I just... spent the night in a hedge, having been thrown through the window of a shitty bar in Birkenhead by a fella on a mobility scooter. I'm fine... ish."

Phil shakes his head and exhales deeply, either in frustration or to breathe away the stench that is presumably coming off me.

"Right. Well, at least go to the toilets and try and clean yourself up, will you?"

"Aye aye, skipper," I reply, saluting him sarcastically as I walk away.

*

In the toilets, I spend a good fifteen minutes evacuating a foul-smelling, greasy, stinging load of slurry from my bowels, and another fifteen gently soaking the bog roll on my face with warm water before slowly peeling it all, bit by bit, off the wounds. A few of them reopen as I do so, and I have to apply pressure from some damp paper towels to stem the fresh flow of blood, but I'm relieved and surprised to see that none of them are especially deep. There'll probably be some sort of light scarring from some of them, and I may have to go and see a plastic surgeon at some point but, right now, just getting through, hour by hour, is the best I can hope for.

It's nearly ten o'clock by the time I actually sit down at my desk, and by now my stomach is starting to growl. The greasy evacuation has left me feeling hollow, and I start thinking about lunch. Specifically, I have a craving for a cheese sandwich. I know I won't be able to justify going out yet so I down the last of my bottle of water, hoping it'll fill me up for the time being, and, as a change of pace, try to focus on work.

An hour later, Phil bursts into my office without warning.

"For fuck's sake," I mutter, louder than I meant to, but no longer really caring. As ever, he places himself at the side of my desk. "Hello again, Phil," I say facetiously. I turn to my left and, sure enough, there's his fucking dick, practically resting atop my desk, mere inches away from my fucking face.

"Okay, Gary," he says, formally, "we need to have a serious talk, I think."

I decide to simply ignore the cunt, turn back to my monitor, and recommence typing.

"Gary," he says after a few seconds. "Did you hear me?"

Again I ignore him, and begin typing more loudly.

"Gary? Gary, can you answer me, please, we need to talk."

Now I'm just smacking my keys exaggeratedly, not actually typing, just making as much noise as I can, shaking my head like Stevie Wonder having a seizure, my tongue flapping around outside my mouth.

"Gary! This is very unprofessional. Gary!"

"Get your fucking dick out me face, Phil," I say quietly, still looking at the screen.

"What?! Gary, what did you just—"

I now stand up and step towards him, my face right next to his. "I SAID. GET. YOUR. FUCKING. BALLS. OUT. OF. MY. FUCKING... MOUTH! PHIL!"

"Gary, that... that doesn't even make sense. Can I... what are you –"

"I would like to go through a day, just one fucking day, *PHIL*, without you coming into my fucking office and swinging your fucking penis inches from my fucking face while I'm trying to fucking work. Is that fucking possible, do you think? Could you see your way clear, Phil, to keeping your genitals out of the vicinity of my fucking face for one single fucking day?"

He looks like he's unsure whether to cry or punch me. After a few deep breaths, he opts for neither. "Right. Okay,

I can see you're not in a very positive mind-set this morning."

"Oh, I'm fucking positive, Phillip... I'm positive I've had enough of my face being closer to your cock than it has ever been to mine."

"Alright, Gary. You've made your point. But, we will be having a very serious talk about your position at this company, and –"

"Oh, you know what? Do what you fucking want. If you're gonna fucking sack me, or get Eddie to, then just fucking do it. Until then, I'm gonna keep coming in and keep picking up my paycheque until I'm told otherwise. But right now, I'm hungry. I smell. I'm hungover to fuck, and I want a fucking cheese sandwich."

I put on my jacket and leave Phil alone in my office as I head out onto the street and to the coffee shop. It's busy when I get there, occupied apparently by just about every fucking beard snood cunt in Liverpool. This must be where they all come to discuss their favourite fucking penny-farthing wax or some such shite. I walk over to the sandwich display, which is situated beneath a hand-painted sign that boasts how all sandwiches are made daily on the premises. I scan the display, wanting nothing more complex but no less satisfying than a cheese sandwich. Instead I find every type of stone-baked, artisan, focaccia, ciabatta, soft tortilla wrap, sweet fucking brioche bread with every bastard type of pulled fucking pork, peri-peri chicken, Moroccan falafel, Cypriot fucking halloumi with all conceivable types of rocket, alfalfa shitting sprouts and sun-bleached cunting tomatoes but nowhere is there a simple cheese fucking sandwich. I storm up to the counter where

The Knobhead is reading a copy of some local arts scene magazine.

"Oh, hey, man," he says when he spots me approaching. "Don't normally see you here this time of—"

"I need a fucking cheese sandwich!" I shout. He drops his paper and steps back defensively. I sense a few ears pricking up and conversations ceasing.

"Erm, yeah, sure, the sandwiches are all over—"

"I know where the fucking sandwiches are, I've just spent an hour reading through their many ingredients. There's no cheese sandwiches, though. I want a cheese sandwich. Is that too much to ask? Or too fucking little, should I say?"

"Whoa, dude," a voice from behind me chirps up. I turn around to see a bearded, tattooed young fucker at the table nearest to me. "There's no need for that, man. We're all just chilling here, and you're being kinda –"

"FUCK YOUR MONOCLE, CUNT!!"

If he was wearing a monocle it probably would have dropped out at this point, but he shuts his mouth and I turn back to the proprietor.

"Right. I want. A cheese. Sandwich. I don't want fucking French brie. I don't want Spanish fucking Manchego, I don't want fucking Cypriot bastard fucking halloumi. I want fucking cheddar. I don't even want mature cheddar. I want the blandest, plainest fucking cheddar there is. I want fucking Netto's own brand, mild fucking cheddar. The kind that's about as fucking flavourful as the fucking plastic it's wrapped in. And I don't want it on stone-baked seeded bread, I don't want it in a fucking wrap. I don't want it in a grilled cunting panini. I want white bread. Plain, bleachy,

176

fucking chemical filled, flavourless as fuck, mass produced fucking white bread. I WANT SLICED FUCKING MIGHTY-WHITE BREAD! And I want fucking shite margarine on it. Not fair trade fucking humanely produced butter. I WANT FUCKING VITALITE! DO YOU FUCKING HEAR ME, YOU FUCKING CRAFT HIPSTER FUCK?"

By now everyone in the café is booing and heckling me. I turn towards them.

"You can all get fucked, you self-absorbed bunch of fucking posers. All your fucking beard oil won't do you any fucking favours when the nuclear fucking holocaust strikes!"

"Right, man. I think that's enough," The Knobhead finally says. "I think you'd better leave. And don't come back. Your negative vibes aren't needed in here, man."

"I'm fucking going, you can shove your fancy fucking sandwiches and your delicious fucking coffee."

I swear I see a genuine twinkle of gratitude when I say his coffee is delicious, before I slam the door shut.

Round the corner I go, heading, without conscious thought, in only one direction. To only one place. The only place I know I can go. The only place I'll be welcome. I get to my destination and press the buzzer, holding it down for several seconds then quickly following it with several short blasts. The door is buzzed open without any sound on the intercom. I bound up the stairs three at a time. I burst into the studio, where Craig is sat back at his desk, omnipresent can in his hand. He looks me up and down, and for the first time ever, seems lost for words.

"Whatever it is," I say, holding my hands up before he can summon any up, "whatever it is you're doing. I want in. Whatever it is you're planning. I want in."

He smiles at me, finishes his can and throws it behind his head. He walks towards me and places a firm hand on each shoulder. "Gary," he says, "welcome to Operation Scat-Bomb."

"Operation Scat-Bomb?"

He smiles again, and nods. "That's right, Gary. Operation Scat-Bomb."

NINETEEN

"We choose our targets carefully," Craig says. "Only the most deserving cases will be targeted."

"And you're sure nobody's gonna get hurt?"

"Well, I suppose that depends on what you mean by 'hurt'. I mean, nobody's gonna get physically harmed in the traditional sense of the word. We're not the fucking Unabomber, Gaz."

"Right, okay." I stand up and pace around the studio. "Okay."

"Gary."

"What?"

"Don't fucking fanny out on me now. It's gonna be fine. Trust me, I've been planning this for a good while now. Don't worry your pretty, messed-up little head about it. Alright?"

"Yeah. Alright."

"That doesn't sound very convincing, mate."

"No, it's fine. I'm on board. Definitely. It's not that."

"What is it then?" Craig asks.

"It's every other fucking thing."

"What every other fucking thing?"

"Fucking work. After what I said to Phil earlier, I'll be lucky to be able to go back to the job I hate. And then there's Jenny. I've got to come up with some sort of explanation as to why I look the way I do, why I didn't come home. Why I smell like the inside of an anus. What the fuck am I gonna tell her? At this rate, I'm likely to be homeless, single and unemployed before the day's through."

"Gary. For fuck's sake. Go home. Fucking apologise for being such a difficult and weird cunt. Promise to try and do better. Then actually *try* to do better. Be honest, don't fucking lie, and hope it's enough. If it's not, *then* you can start to worry about being single and homeless."

"Surprisingly sage-like relationship advice for someone who makes porn for a living."

"And without doubt the best advice you've received so far."

"Yeah, Probably. And what about work? What about fucking Phil?"

"You let me worry about fucking Phil," he says enigmatically. I've got no idea what he's talking about, but I decide his advice on the first issue is pretty sound, so I head home to attempt to act on it.

*

When I get back to the flat Jenny is sitting on the couch, reading. She turns her head halfway to look at me as I enter the living room.

"You're back then, are you?" she says, and turns back before doing a double-take. She looks me up and down, grimacing at the state of me. "Fuck me, Gary," she says, "what the fucking hell happened to you?" She walks round the couch to me and reaches up to the cuts on my face, grabs at my dishevelled clothes, then recoils when the smell hits her. "Jesus, have you been rolling around in fox shit or something?"

"Quite possibly," I say,

"Gary, this isn't funny. What the fuck happened to you? Where have you been? What the fuck's going on? You'd better start fucking talking to me, Gary."

And I do. I talk to her. We sit on the couch and I tell her everything that happened last night, every single detail. Through tears and pleas for mercy, I lay it all on the line, from my anxiety attack upon leaving work, the spontaneous decision to go into The Vernon, right through to crashing out of Moodz and vomiting all over McDonald's, to my first ever night of rough sleeping, right through to my storming out of work. I even tell her that I've been seeing Craig, which feels oddly like confessing to an affair. I decide to leave out the kidnapping.

When I'm done, an uneasy truce is reached. Surprisingly, the fact that I've been spending time with Craig seems to be causing more concern than the fact that I drank like I was trying to kill myself, and nearly was killed by being shoved through a window.

"Why is that such a concern?" I say.

"I'm not sure. I mean, I know that I sort of owe him a bit. If he hadn't given you that push, you might never have actually called me back. But, that being said, he does seem to cause... well... fucking bedlam wherever he goes. I dunno. It's not as though you have many friends of your own. Maybe having him back around will be good for you. I'm just not sure."

"No, neither am I, if I'm honest. It could be good, it could be disastrous."

"And he makes porn?"

"Yeah," I nod. "Basically. Well, not basically. He makes porn."

Jenny nods too. "That's a bit... weird? Isn't it?"

"Suppose so, yeah. But not so much for Craig."

"No," Jenny says, "I suppose it isn't. He's not gonna try and get you to shag a porn star or anything, is he?"

"I very much doubt he'd even consider me capable. And I think porn *star* would overstate the status of the participants involved. And I think we both know you don't really need to worry about me taking him up on it even if he does."

"No. Well, maybe, unless and until he does anything to make us think otherwise, let's look at him being back around as a good thing, shall we?"

*

The next morning, I'm back into routine, for now at least. Jenny came back into the bedroom, and I make the usual walk into work, minus the stop off for coffee, of course. I briefly consider hiding round the corner and asking someone to go in and purchase one for me, like a thirteen-year-old asking a passing adult to buy them fags and cider, but quickly dismiss the idea partly on the grounds of how pathetic it would be, but mainly because it would necessitate me talking to a stranger. Instead I buy a coffee from another outlet a few roads down. It's good coffee, in fact it's very good coffee, but it's not even close to the other one. I'm briefly overcome with regret at my actions, but this is quickly replaced by rage at the injustice of my barring.

My brief detour means I'm a few minutes late for work, and when I get there there's a strange atmosphere evident. Nobody seems to be working, instead they're all standing around their own or each other's work stations, all looking very concerned about something. Some are holding their hands over their mouths in shock, and there's a low hum of agitated voices.

Instead of heading into my own office, I hang around the main office space, eager to know what's happened. I wonder whether somebody has died, and if so who? And then I wonder whether I'd really care.

I look towards Eddie's office and he's in there with Phil. Eddie is looking a bit shell-shocked as Phil paces frantically around, talking into his mobile. I take a few steps closer and can pick up his half of the phone conversation.

"Look, this is bullshit, yeah? Total fucking bullshit!" he's shouting. "Yeah, I know it was from my email and my Facebook, I already said... well I don't know, do I? If I knew that, then we wouldn't... WHAT?!?! YOU'VE GOT TO BE FUCKING KIDDING ME?! Oh come on, Anthony, this is just... yes, of course I understand the gravity of the situation... FUCK! BULLSHIT! BULLSHIT!"

I approach a small group gathered by a computer. They nod to acknowledge me as I reach them.

"Hey," one of them says.

"Alright. What the fuck's going on? What's up with Phil?"

"You haven't heard?" another one of them asks.

"No, I've just got in. What's happened?"

They start snickering uncomfortably, like a bunch of nine-year-olds who've just heard their first dick joke.

"Well," the first one says, "when we all got in this morning, we all had an email from Phil."

"And?"

"Well, it had an attachment with it."

They all start laughing again.

"Yes? And? What was the attachment?"

He leans in a bit closer.

"He'd sent us all a picture of his cock."

"He what?!"

"Seriously man, his cock. All our screens were suddenly filled by a fucking close up of Phil's hard-on. Seems he's sent the same picture to everyone in his address book. Including women and everyone at head office. That's who he's on the phone to now."

I remember Craig's cryptic words yesterday before I left his studio.

You leave fucking Phil to me.

"You don't fucking say." I'm smiling now as I turn back to Phil and tune back into his voice.

"What?! WITH IMMEDIATE EFFECT?! FUCK!!"

He throws his phone across Eddie's office, storms out and heads towards his own office.

"Fucking crock of shit. Fucking bullshit, man. Total fucking bullshit," he's saying to nobody in particular as he picks up his cycle helmet. "Fuck this place, anyway. Waste of my fucking time. Bunch of amateurs," he's saying as he emerges and heads towards the exit.

"You still want that report actioning, Phil?" I ask. He ignores me and heads towards the stairs.

"Don't forget your yoghurt," I shout to him. He stops and heads towards the kitchenette, before turning back towards the door.

"Fuck it!" he shouts. As he reaches the top of the stairs he turns towards me. I smile and wave. He narrows his eyes at me and looks like he's about to say something but I turn my wave into a "wanker" gesture, and in an instant, he goes from enraged to deflated, and heads down the stairs and out of view.

*

I'm picking a few items off the shelf in the Tesco Metro in town before I head home, namely toiletries and cleaning products, and a loaf of bread. I'm weighing up the best wipe-to-penny value ratio on two packs of wipes when I hear a voice.

"Gary?"

I recognise the voice, and know who it is before I even turn my head.

"Hello, Gary," Brian says.

"Hello, Brian," I respond, in a tone of voice oddly akin to that of a scorned ex-lover.

"How are you, Gary? How've you been? I haven't seen you since... well..."

"Since you made a terrible professional decision to force me off benefits and into a shitty job at some fuck-awful call centre, leading to a catastrophic sequence of events that nearly destroyed me? Since then?"

"I... I did what I felt was for the best, Gary. My intentions were only ever to –"

"To help massage the unemployment statistics? Either forcing me into work, or forcing me to fucking kill myself, it's one less person claiming benefits, isn't it, Bri?"

"Gary," he looks genuinely upset. "I'd never deliberately put anyone at risk."

"Well, intentionally or not, that's what happened."

He looks around awkwardly, his eyes settling briefly on the contents of my basket, a quizzical expression appearing on his face as he notices the various different types of cleaning wipes.

"I'm... I'm sorry that any choices or decisions I made had any negative impact on you, Gary. I truly am."

He waits a moment, perhaps expecting me to accept his apology, but I don't say a word.

"How are you now?" he says when it's clear he's not going to find the forgiveness he presumably hoped to be granted when he saw me on the cleaning products aisle. I shrug my shoulders.

"Okay," I say. "I'm living with Jenny. I think I told you about her the one time I came to see you after starting at the call centre. We've got a flat over this side of the water."

"You're *living* with her?" Brian doesn't seem compelled to hide his incredulity now he's no longer bound by the rules of professional conduct. "Well, that's fantastic, Gary. Great news. Are you working?"

"Yeah, I'm working at a... erm... company."

"What sort of company?"

"Oh, erm, well, media and that. You know, design stuff and... that."

"And what are you doing there?"

"Well, it's hard to explain. Social media stuff, mostly."

"Well, Gary, this is great news. You're holding down a job, you're in a relationship. Just brilliant."

"Yeah, alright. Don't be trying to take any sort of sly fucking credit for any of this, Brian. Whatever place I'm at, it's nothing to do with your decision. Anything good that may have happened is *despite* what you did, not because of it. So if you're thinking of saying 'told you so' or taking any sort of smug professional satisfaction, fucking forget it. Don't be going off telling your colleagues about some victory you think you've had or writing some shit paper on me."

He's holding his hands up to stop my flow. "Gary, I'm not in that field anymore, mental health, I mean. I left that line of work a couple of years ago."

"Well, that's probably for the best, given what I know about your fucking methods. What are you doing now?"

"I decided to get back into teaching."

He says "back" as though he expected me to have a clue or give a shit about what he did before, neither of which are the case.

"Teaching? Christ, you can mess up the heads of entire classrooms full of people instead of one on one, then, eh?"

He seems to take this as a joke, which it isn't, and gives a little chuckle.

"Well, Gary," he says, "I'd best leave you to it, I suppose. It was good to see you."

He offers me his hand to shake, and I stare at it for a moment before giving a handshake that is lame even by my standards. I turn away from him without saying goodbye, and back to the shelf. I can feel him linger at my shoulder for a moment before he finally walks away. I continue to weigh the benefits, cleaning ability wise and economy wise, of two separate packs of wipes, but find myself deadlocked between the two.

"For fuck's sake," I say aloud, before dropping my basket to the floor and running out of the store. As I get outside I stop and look around, towards Church Street, and down towards Williamson Square, but I can't see Brian anywhere.

I go back into Tesco and finish my shopping.

*

"Couldn't you have got some thicker gloves than this? Like washing-up gloves or something?"

"Oh fuck off, Gary," Craig replies as we dump another bag into the back of his van. "I've got you a fucking boiler suit, a mask to cover your mouth and some fucking surgical gloves. That shit isn't fucking cheap, you know."

"I know it's not," I say, "and I appreciate the thought with the boiler suit, it's just... the gloves are a bit thin, that's all. My skin is physically too close to the shit. I'd prefer either a thicker glove or another layer of protection."

"Another fucking layer? Gary, you've got three fucking pairs of surgical gloves on. Fucking colorectal surgeons literally hold cancerous bowel in their fucking hands with a single pair of these things on, and you're fucking pissing and moaning coz you're worried about touching a bit of cow shit? You're not even picking it up with your fucking hands. You're using a fucking spade. Which I bought for you. And collecting it into a thick bag. Your hands, even your *gloved* hands, don't come into contact with, or anywhere fucking near to, any of the shit at any fucking point. Fucking quit being such a fanny, for fuck's sake."

"Look, Craig, this is not something I normally do, okay? I know you've sunk to such depths of utter fucking depravity that this is probably nothing to you, but shovelling up cow pats in a fucking cold field in the middle of the night is not my idea of a good fucking time."

"And you think it's mine? I've got plenty of places I'd rather be, but this is a necessary fucking evil, okay? Now get fucking shovelling, or spading or whatever. We're nearly done now."

"Yeah, alright."

"What did you tell Jenny about where you were going, anyway?"

"I made something up about an audit in work."

"An audit, eh? So you lied to her, then?"

I stop shovelling/spading and nod.

"Not sure it's a great idea for you to start lying to her, mate."

"What the fuck else could I do? Tell her the truth? Tell her I was driving off to a field in Cheshire to collect animal shite with my ex-convict friend?"

"I dunno, maybe. I've never met the woman, just seen her tight little arse through your window that one time, but maybe she'd be more supportive than you'd think. Who the fuck knows?"

"Craig, she's *beyond* supportive. I mean, can you imagine how difficult it must be, living with someone like me?"

"I'd rather not, I stayed with you for less than a week, and I can honestly say I was more relaxed in prison."

"Exactly, well she has to put up with me full fucking time. That takes a lot of patience. That takes someone incredibly supportive. But she's got limits. Everyone has."

"You know best, mate. Oh no, actually you know fuck all. But whatever, if you wanna poison your relationship by becoming a duplicitous cunt as well as a needy, high-as-fuck maintenance one, be my fucking guest."

He throws another bag into the van and slams the door shut. "Right, let's get out of here before we get mistaken for a couple of fucking badger baiters or something."

TWENTY

The Knobhead looks particularly pleased with himself today. That's unsurprising, given that, at three o'clock in the afternoon, his establishment is full of patrons, all ordering multiple cups of over-priced coffee, sandwiches and pastries, and generally *"chillaxing"* as though they have no intention of leaving this place any time soon. They must have money to burn. I see one young man heading back to the counter to order an extra-large coffee, having already consumed two. It never ceases to amaze me that, in a time of great economic uncertainty, with living standards stagnating in real terms, these young hipster types seem to be able to sit around in coffee shops and cereal cafés spending endless sums of money on expensive coffee whilst apparently having no source of income, if the time they spend in places like this in the middle of the working day is anything to go by. I can only imagine they're some sort of trust fund kids, and don't have any need to seek gainful employment, and choose to use their privilege to cultivate a sort of bohemian image for themselves, when they stand to inherit millions once their parents cark it or they hit thirty.

"Here we go," Craig says.

We're sitting opposite the Bean Grinder in Craig's van. The windows are blacked out slightly, so we're able to observe at close quarters without being detected, and the zoom facility on Craig's camera gives us an even clearer view inside. He taps me on the shoulder and points to a delivery driver getting out of his van about a hundred yards down the street. The driver checks the address on the large cardboard box he's struggling to carry and checks out the addresses of a few other places before spotting Bean Grinder. He carries the box into the shop and I feel a strange tingle of excitement, which I'm sure Craig shares if the punch on the arm he gives me is anything to go by. The Knobhead steps out from behind the counter to sign for the box before the delivery driver helps him to place it on a table.

"Come on, you bearded clown," Craig says, as he switches on the camera he has set up on the dashboard.

The driver has gone now and The Knobhead stands in front of the box on one of the few vacant tables, front and centre of the café. He begins to open it but a customer approaches the counter, so he abandons the box to go and serve him.

"For fuck's sake," Craig spits, "let him get his own fucking Frappuccino, you daft prick. Open the cunting box."

"Craig, maybe we shouldn't go through with this," I say quietly. He turns away from the camera and looks at me.

"Oh shut up, you flaccid penis," he says. "You really think now is the time for an attack of conscience? Besides, exactly how are you gonna alter our course now? Stroll in there and explain the situation to him?"

"I suppose not."

"Of course not. Plus, do you actually *want* to stop this? I mean, if you really do, then feel free, I'm not gonna stop you. But *do* you?"

I shift uncomfortably in the passenger seat. "No. Not really."

"Great, now shut the fuck up and let's enjoy the fucking show, shall we?"

I nod and turn back to the coffee shop while Craig lowers his head back down to the camera and zooms in, muttering quiet encouragements.

"Go on you fucking pomade-stinking twat, open your fucking present. OH, GET TO FUCK!" he shouts as yet another customer orders a coffee, keeping beardy behind the counter. "How can these people drink so much fucking coffee? Don't they know caffeine's bad for you? They must be more wired than a fucking TV executive after a coke binge. Oh, hang on... here we go."

Once again, The Knobhead steps out from behind the counter and walks back to the table upon which the box is resting. He looks at it with the kind of dumb curiosity with which an elderly dog might regard a new and unfamiliar object that's just appeared in its house. He slowly peels back the masking tape and opens the first flap.

"Go on, fucking open it," Craig implores him.

He opens the second flap and... nothing happens.

"FUCKING BASTARD!" Craig shouts. "IT DIDN'T WORK!"

We look back to the coffee shop but Craig's rant and our view inside are both interrupted by the sight and sound of something slapping hard against the glass. Behind the elaborate logo on the window we can see only brown. There is a moment of silence before we hear the screams. Seconds later the door to Bean Grinder bursts open and a dozen shit-covered hipsters trip over each other in the race to evacuate the building. Several end up in the gutter, trying in vain to wipe the shit from their eyes, out of their hair. A young man in a flat cap is on his hands and knees as he spits and vomits out a mouthful of mixed human and animal crap. Craig is struggling to hold his camera straight as he contorts with laughter. His amusement only increases as, finally, we catch sight of The Knobhead staggering out into the street looking like a zombie emerging from the toilet ditch at a 1960s music festival. Though his customers are pretty caked, he's clearly taken the brunt of the hit, desperately trying to pull the faeces out of his beard with his fingers, which are also covered in shit. His customers begin to scatter, people on the street dodging out of the path of this shit-stinking exodus.

"Wait!" he shouts after them. "Don't leave!"

As though the idea of yet another espresso will outweigh the fact that the premises now look like the world's greatest dirty protest has been staged in there.

"Right, hood up," Craig says as he starts the engine of his van.

We pull up our hoods as we pull off the curb, drive over to the other side of the street and stop outside the scene of devastation. Craig winds the window down and extends a gloved hand to our victim.

"Take a card," he says.

The Knobhead says nothing, still in shock, but slowly reaches out and takes it anyway. He turns it over and looks at the logo on the front.

YOU'VE BEEN VISITED BY OPERATION SCATBOMB
Stop being a cunt.

"Tell your friends about us," Craig says, before driving us away.

*

We park around the back of Craig's studio and run inside. I double over, struggling for breath.

"What... what's wrong with me?" I say, barely managing to get my words out.

"Wrong with you?"

"Yeah... can't... can't fucking breathe hardly."

"Gary..."

"And this fucking... pain... in my fucking chest and guts, what is it? Is this a panic attack or a fucking heart attack or what?"

"Gary?"

"What? What's wrong with me?"

"There's nothing wrong with you, mate. Nothing at all."

"Then why can't I fucking breathe properly?"

"Because you're laughing, you fucking prick."

"Huh?"

"Gary, you haven't stopped laughing since the scat-bomb went off. I've never seen you laugh so much. I'm not sure I've ever seen anyone laugh so much."

I manage to stand up almost straight and take some deep breaths and my breathing begins to steady. "Fuck," I say. "I've really been laughing all that time?"

"Like a fucking hyena on spice, my weird friend."

"Jesus. Well, that was... good! That worked well. But... it's not really a scat-*bomb*, though, is it?"

"What?" Craig takes a can from the fridge and passes one to me.

"Well," I continue as I open the can and take a swig, "it's something that's been bothering me since you told me the plan."

"Go on."

"The word 'bomb' suggests an explosion, as though the shit is being dispersed by an incendiary element, right?"

"Yeah. So? What the fuck you getting at?"

"The device you built, it's more a case of it *propelling* the shit out, right? The spring-loaded thing propels the shit out. Don't get me wrong, it's really well designed and everything, it worked far better than I imagined, it's just, you know... it's not *technically* a bomb. Is it?"

"Well, you're technically a fucking bell-end. Alright then, it's a fucking *Crapapult*. You happy now, you pedantic fucking prick?"

I start laughing again as the image of the shit-stained coffee lovers flashes through my mind, but this time I stop short of full-blown hysterics.

"So," Craig says, "you up for more of this?"

I nod my head without hesitation. "I am."

"Good, you get thinking about who our next target should be. Think big, okay?"

I nod again, a dozen possible targets already entering my mind.

"Now fuck off, I've got a scene to shoot in a bit."

Craig downs the rest of his can and disappears into a backroom, where I can hear him fucking about with some camera equipment.

"Right," I shout through to him. "I'll see you... soon then."

I hear some sort of affirmative grunt, and let myself out. As I hit the street, the laughter may have subsided but my heart is still pounding, adrenaline racing through my veins. I check my watch; Jenny should be back at the flat in about fifteen minutes. I turn and head for home.

*

When I get to the flat Jenny is in the kitchen, leaning against the kitchen table and texting on her phone. She looks up as I enter.

"You're home a bit early aren't you? Everything alri—"

She doesn't get to finish the sentence as I grab her and kiss her hard. She pulls away after a few seconds and looks at me, understandably confused by my actions, before moving back into the kiss. I rip her blouse open, relieved not to receive a slap for popping the buttons off, and, after a few seconds of trying unsuccessfully to take her bra off (a skill I *still* haven't come close to mastering), I pull it over her head and throw it away. I grab a tit in each hand and squeeze them as Jenny begins to undo my trousers and take my shirt off, and I suck on her nipples as she takes my already granite-hard cock out and starts wanking it. I pull down her trousers and knickers, managing to pull them over the shoe on one leg, but they get stuck on the other shoe and I struggle for a few seconds to get the offending shoe off and Jenny is now naked except for one rogue sock. I lift her up onto the table and kneel in front of her and start frenziedly licking her out, like a starving man desperately trying to tongue out the remaining oil inside an empty bag of crisps. This is something I've only done a few times, but right now the taste

197

of Jenny is the greatest thing I've ever experienced, and I bury my face between her legs as though I'm trying to actually get my entire face inside her vagina, like I want to tunnel inside her, my tongue entering into her like a sand snake burrowing its way through a desert. She grabs my hair and wraps her legs around my head, using them to push my face further in as she bucks and grinds her cunt against my mouth and face like a monkey scratching its arse against a tree, until she comes, hard. She lifts me up and drops to her knees and sucks my cock but I want to be inside her, so I lift her back onto the table and she guides me into her and I fuck her hard and fast, her perfect tits jiggling as she leans back, and I grab them and hold them still as I rub my face on them, trying to envelope my head within them as much as possible, Jenny's legs now wrapped tightly round my waist, adding more force to my already frenetic thrusting. She stops me and pushes me back. Whether it was her intention or not, I fall backwards onto the kitchen floor and Jenny practically takes a gymnasts leap off the table, executing a perfect landing directly onto my cock, and rides me as I take turns to reach up and grab her tits and hold her arse as she lifts up and down. I feel my orgasm beginning to build from the soles of my feet, and Jenny senses it.

"Are you ready?" she says.

"Nearly."

She increases her speed, and positions herself so she too begins to tense as her own orgasm builds. I manage to match her rhythm and thrust as she moves, the two of us now in perfect synchronisation, until we come together, me shooting what feels like endless jets of semen into her. I come so hard I'm surprised she doesn't fly off me on the end of a fire hose of spunk. She drops on top of me, both of us breathless.

*

A while later, after we've had less frenzied but no less enjoyable sex again on the kitchen floor, and showered together, we're lying in bed, exhausted.

"So are you gonna tell me what the fuck prompted that?" Jenny asks.

"It's hard to explain," I say, already dozing off.

"I mean, I'm not complaining or anything. It was just... unexpected."

"I know."

"So, what happened?"

"I just feel a bit... invigorated by something."

"By what?"

Jenny's voice is slowing down now, and she's sounding drowsy.

"Well, just a project I've got going on."

"With work?" she says through a massive yawn.

I wait a moment before responding, and Jenny's lack of follow-up question tells me she's on the verge of sleep. I offer a vague, non-committal "mm-hmm", and no further questions are forthcoming. I turn away and onto my back and close my eyes. I instantly feel myself falling asleep, satisfied that I've managed to avoid any more difficult questions for now, without having had to lie.

TWENTY-ONE

"Right, so... er, we're all probably a bit, like, shocked about the whole, ya know, er, Phil situation, yeah?"

Eddie has called us all into the "ideas room" for a meeting and he's manfully trying to navigate us through the rocky waters of what everyone in the office has dubbed *"sextgate"*. He's trying his best and is failing fairly spectacularly, even adding unnecessary inverted commas with his fingers at the word "situation". He goes on to tell us in his own meandering way that he has (before his first line of the day kicks in), that Phil has been suspended pending investigation, and that several female employees at head office are apparently taking legal advice and are considering bringing private sexual harassment suits against him in light of his obscene messages.

Most of the office seems fairly indifferent to the "situation", seeing the whole thing as more amusing than anything else. A few make shocked noises but clearly don't really have an opinion, but I can tell, though he's trying to seem all concerned, shocked and paternal about it all, Eddie is secretly delighted. For now, at least, he's free to go on running the place in his own lacklustre way until another consultant/trouble-shooter/meddling cunt gets sent up to ask why he's paying talentless frauds like me a more-than-reasonable wage. His barely concealed delight is nothing, of course, compared with the 50/50 mix of jubilation and relief I'm currently feeling.

"Right everyone, erm, thanks for coming in today. I mean, I know you were in anyway, ya know, coz you all work here, but I mean, thanks for coming to this meeting."

Eddie seems a bit slow this morning, more so than usual, even. Presumably he's forgotten to take his morning espresso/cocaine cocktail. His phone bleeps and vibrates loudly on the desk he's standing next to. He picks it up and smiles as he reads the message and begins typing a response before seemingly realising where he is, closing his phone cover and putting it back in his pocket.

"Erm, so, yeah," he continues, slowly. "The reason I wanted you all to come in here was that, well, head office, and me too, like, well, we thought we should have a kind of, like an open forum purification session." He recites these last three words as though the first time he heard them together or individually was whilst on the phone to head office a few minutes ago, which I'm certain is the case, "about this whole... er... Phil thing, yeah?"

"*Philth*, you mean," someone says, to a few hoots of laughter.

"Phil McCrackin," someone else offers before a pause followed by a cessation of laughter. Clearly two crap puns on Phil's name are all that this company full of vibrant young creatives were capable of.

"Phil Shameson," someone eventually reluctantly chimes in. I don't get the joke but someone helpfully points out that Phil's surname is Jameson. Understanding the joke doesn't make it any funnier.

"It's not fucking funny," a female voice shouts from near the back of the room. As I was unsurprised to learn, our company is typical among tech- and media-centric firms like ours in being disproportionately understaffed by women. "What Phil did was criminal. It was harassment. It's the kind of thing men like him have been getting away with for centuries, and it's not a laughing matter."

The room goes quiet as all the laughter stops, and people nod their head in agreement or look down at the ground in embarrassment at having made light of the whole affair.

I recognise that the women – and probably men too – that I work with will have been subjected to genuine pain or revulsion when Craig somehow framed Phil as the mid-level media firm's equivalent of Harvey Weinstein. I also recognise that, as a result of Craig's actions on my behalf, a man's career is probably ruined. He may be vociferously denying any wrongdoing, but there is no doubt that, post #MeToo, there is no coming back for Phil. Phil is finished. Phil is fucked. And for that, I can honestly say I feel no remorse, no fucking regret whatsoever. Fuck him. With his physique, supreme confidence and overwhelming sense of innate entitlement, that cunt was a fucking sex crime waiting to happen, if he didn't have a string of them on his CV already. By ruining the fucker's life now, we've probably saved a dozen women from any number of grotty office passes, corridor arse-grabs or far, far worse. But even with that knowledge, I do recognise that, for my gain, some women have been made to suffer, and I feel far worse about it than I would have anticipated. I suppose I'm beginning to learn to understand that my actions, or, in this case, actions committed on my behalf, have consequences. But while I recognise this, I quickly decide that any actual suffering that may have been caused is, given the direct benefit to myself, more than acceptable collateral damage.

"Yeah, absolutely," Eddie, who I'd forgotten was even meant to be leading this meeting, carries on. "What Phil did was totally unacceptable and out of order. But, I mean, he's gone now, right? So we can get back to normal, get back to doing what we do, yeah?"

He's starting to sound as though his grasp of what we do is as loose as mine. He wraps things up and sends us back to "express ourselves", which I do by popping an extra Amitriptyline and giving my desk an extra clean.

*

After dinner, me and Jenny are on the couch. I'm reading while Jenny watches the local news. I've tuned it out as background noise but my ears tune instantly back in when the newsreader says, *"... and now we go to a bizarre story about an attack on a city centre coffee shop..."*

I peer over the top of my magazine and see shaky footage of the outside of Bean Grinder, a caption bar underneath reading: *"'Dirty' attack on café causes damage and sickness"*.

I glance sideways to gauge Jenny's reaction but she's just displaying the kind of reaction one would expect from someone watching this report. The programme has moved from the studio to the video footage from the scene, a reporter looking deeply concerned as he speaks to the camera.

"The Bean Grinder was, as always, full of customers when the bizarre attack took place late yesterday afternoon. What has been described as some sort of explosive or possible propulsive device was detonated, spraying customers and staff with faecal matter. The café had to be closed for decontamination –"

The next line is drowned out as Jenny bursts out laughing. "Oh, fucking hell! I shouldn't laugh. I mean, it's awful, really, isn't it."

"Hmm?" I say, as though I'm too engrossed in the Gary Kasparov interview I've been pretending to read to have heard what she's said.

"Someone blew up some sort of shit bomb at some poncey coffee shop in town," she says, trying to cover her laughter with shock.

"Oh yeah?" I reply, trying to stealthily look over the top of the mag.

"Police claim the attack is not terror-related," the report continues.

"Terror-related?" Jenny shouts at the TV. "Of course it's not terror-related. Not unless ISIS are seriously changing tack."

"Mm-hmm," I mumble, for fear that if I say anything more than that my voice will crack and betray me.

The report from the scene of the crime ends and switches back to the studio.

"Nobody has yet claimed credit for the attack, though we've obtained an image of a card that was left at the scene. The card contains language that viewers may find offensive…"

I glance up again and see the screen filled by the card we left, the word *cunt* appearing on local news for probably the first time. I notice that Jenny's chuckling has now ceased completely, and turn my eyes to the side to see she is doing exactly the same thing to me. I decide I have to quickly use diversion tactics before any latent suspicion becomes active suspicion.

"You should have a read of this Kasparov interview, you know. Interesting stuff."

"Mm-hmm," she says, taking over grunting duties from me.

"Anyway, I'm gonna have a shower and go to bed."

"Gary?" she says before I reach the door.

"Yeah?" I say, stopping and turning towards her. She's not looking at me but at the TV, a look of confusion on her face, even though the programme has now moved on from the Bean Grinder attack. She narrows her eyes at the screen before shaking her head slightly and unscrewing her face, letting it slip back into a normal expression of tiredness.

"Nothing," she says. "Doesn't matter. See you in a minute."

And I've dodged a bullet there.

TWENTY-TWO

"That's very positive news, Gary," Kate says.

I've been detailing the recent upturn in relations between Jenny and myself, though I leave out the specifics of eating Jenny's cunt like a pig with its snout stuck in a Pringles tube. I also leave out the Crapapult, putting my slightly improved general mood down to an interesting but unspecified project at work. Recycling the same lie that I used on Jenny may be lazy but feels like the least complicated way of explaining things.

"It is," I say, with a note of caution. "I mean, I'm not getting carried away; a reasonable ten days where my anxiety is slightly less and my mood slightly better than usual doesn't exactly make me Matt fucking Haig, but obviously it's a good thing."

"I would like to go back to the meal out with your parents for a moment, though."

"Really? I thought we'd covered that."

"Well, we did, but I think there's a little more to say about it."

"I don't see what," I interrupt hastily but non-aggressively. "I acted the prick, me and Jenny fell out over it, I went a bit Robert Downey Jr. in Birkenhead, me and Jenny made up."

"You did," Kate says, nodding along with each point, "but what I'd like us to understand is *why* you 'acted the prick'."

"Because I'm a bit of a prick sometimes."

"I think there's more to it than that, Gary, and I'd like to understand what that is."

I shrug my shoulders, offering no further insight.

"Was it the fact that Jenny had arranged this behind your back? And that your parents had effectively conspired with her?"

"I dunno. Maybe," I say, conceding a small amount of ground. Kate doesn't say anything in response. "Alright, yes. It was. I deliberately and consciously sabotaged it because I was pissed off with her for arranging it, and with *them* for going along with it."

"Was what Jenny did really so bad?"

"Fuck, yes! She did it because she was pissed off with me, she did it as an act of petty fucking revenge because she knew I was hyper-aware of the delicate situation I was in, and she fucking used that against me to fucking ambush me into doing something that she knows full fucking well is about the worst possible kind of thing to spring on me. And those two miserable old fuckers went along with it coz they think the sun shines out of Jenny's every fucking orifice, and they couldn't give less of a fuck about what an event like that would do to me. In fact, they probably fucking enjoyed making me suffer, the sadistic old cunts. Fuck them. Jenny was bang fucking out of order and I was more than entitled to sabotage the evening like that. My behaviour was entirely justified and, frankly, the more I think about it, the more I believe that. What the fuck was she thinking? Because me and her are in the midst of some petty fucking squabble, she thinks it's in any way fair to throw me into something like that? For what? Some form of fucking revenge? To engage in some vulgar display of fucking power? Fuck her! She can fuck off, Kate. The spiteful fucking bitch!"

I notice that I've been pacing around the room, and that I'm shaking like a shitting dog. I drop to the floor and hold my head in my hands.

"Fucking hell. I don't mean that, Kate. I don't think that about Jenny. Honestly, I don't. I just... I was..."

"You were angry."

"Yeah. I was, but there was no need for –"

"No, but, Gary, you *are* entitled to feel angry. Jenny *did* act unfairly, from what you're telling me. But the way to react to that is not to cause a scene in a restaurant or to say things you don't really mean about Jenny while you're here, although it's certainly better to say those things here than to her. What would have been a more constructive way of addressing the issue, at the time?"

"By talking to her, of course. By calmly, rationally explaining my point of view. I know that, but I'm a long way from being able to do that. My stock response is to become awkward or verbally aggressive. I haven't learned how else to react. Not yet."

"Not yet, you haven't. But you'll get there."

I sit back in my chair and lean back.

"So, it seems I haven't progressed much this last week at all, doesn't it?"

"That's not true, Gary. Progress is being made, believe me. But it's a long-term thing. It won't all be solved after a few positive days."

*

That night I have a horrible dream in which I'm standing on the roof of Bean Grinder. I reach down and start tearing chunks of the roof away with my bare hands. When I've created a hole big enough, I drop a large hose in and watch as it starts pumping gallons of shit into the café below.

"Hey, man," I hear from inside, and rip back more roofing tiles until the hole is big enough for me to poke my head in next to the hose. The shit is already halfway to the ceiling and there, in the middle of it, flailing about trying to stop himself from sinking, is The Knobhead himself.

"Oh, hey," he says to me, "erm, could you, like, maybe gimme a hand, yeah?"

"I can't do that."

"Oh, right. It's just that I'm, like, drowning in shit, yeah? Dunno how it got here."

"It was me. I put it there."

"Oh," he says nodding his head, "why?"

"It's a long story. But it had to be someone, and you were the first person I thought of."

"Not sure I totally deserve this really, tbh."

He's really struggling to stay afloat now. The level of shit seems to have stopped rising but it's getting thicker and more swamp-like. His head periodically drops below the surface for a few second before re-emerging. Despite his desperate plight and his hopeless flapping, he manages to maintain the same laid-back demeanour and laconic drawl whenever he speaks, when he would be entitled to be screaming for help.

"So could you, like, maybe reach down and help me or something?" he asks, as the shit reaches his neck, just his head and a single outstretched hand now visible. I hear a commotion from the other side of the roof. I look over to see Craig, naked and chained to the wall like a shrunken King Kong, wrestling against his binds.

"Get some more fucking shit in there, Gaz. I've got a fat fucking load ready to go. Just aim me arse into that hole and I'll do the rest."

"Uuuuurgh, so, like, a little help would be appreciated here, dude," The Knobhead says, drawing my attention back to him.

"I can't do that."

"Why's that, man?"

"Because you're covered in shit. If I reach down and grab your hand then I'm gonna end up covered in shit too. Even if I put a glove on, pulling you out is likely to mean you'll get shit on my clothes. And even if I manage to avoid that, being in such close proximity to that much shit is just not something I'm willing to countenance. Sorry, but you're on your own."

"Kewl, man, kewl," he says as he disappears below the surface for the last time.

I wake up hyperventilating and covered in sweat. I reach over to my phone and send a text to Craig.

– *We need to pick more deserving targets in future.*

TWENTY-THREE

"Meninists". "Pick up artists". "Men's rights activists".

Of all the online phenomena I've become familiar with during my time with CUltureSHock, this is perhaps one of the most pathetic and baffling. A movement begun and propagated by, for the most part, middle-class(ish) white men who, despite having all the power and privilege in the world, are still so pathetically inadequate that they simply can't cope with women anywhere having any kind of voice or being better at something than they are. They choose to express their feelings of insecurity by anonymously abusing and issuing rape and death threats to any female with anything like a prominent voice online. It doesn't matter what fields they are prominent in; politics, journalism, gaming software, sports or the performing arts. As someone who had always believed himself to be entirely inadequate in every regard imaginable, you'd think I would be one of these people. But even I don't feel the need to shift the blame for my own failings and my pathetic station in life onto women.

As if the gradual rise of this movement, and presumably this is the only rising these impotent bed-wetters will ever be doing, wasn't bad enough, we now have the Incels. "Involuntary Celibates". If you thought the meninists were pathetic pond life, you haven't glimpsed the depths of patheticness and horror humans are capable of plumbing until you've spent a few hours spiralling down this particular rabbit-hole.

Incels are a sub-community of virgins who seem to exist almost entirely on subreddit and 4Chan. These are men who, quite openly within the confines of these online groups, detail their unchosen virginity. They actually seem to want to outdo each other with tales of their desperation. They detail their loneliness, their complete lack of sexual interaction with women. Some of these men are in their 30s and they've never so much as kissed a woman. And guess whose fault it all is? That's right, it's those pesky fucking women again!

There's some truly vile, hateful shit on the internet, and you're only ever a few clicks away from it, but these forums, where men openly boast about cracking one off over news stories about the rapes and murders of women, are as bad as it gets.

So, when discussing with Craig who our next target should be, I was in no doubt.

"Jonah La Verde? Never fucking heard of him."

"Nor had I until a few days ago," I say as I sip a coffee purchased from one of Bean Grinder's rivals and Craig sips from a can of Stella.

"So, who is he?"

"He was born in Toronto in 1988 but was raised in New York," I say, scrolling through his Wikipedia page on Craig's PC. "Wrote his first book, 'Lions, Not Mice' in 2009, followed by 'The Mating Game' in 2013."

"Fucking 'Lions, Not Mice'? 'The Mating Game'? I'd never heard of him until a few minutes ago but I'm gonna fucking enjoy covering this cunt in shite. And people actually pay to listen to him talk?"

"Yeah. He goes on these big speaking tours around America, Europe and Australia where he tells sad, single, women-hating men how to manipulate girls into fucking them."

"And how much do these fucking saddos pay to listen to this crap?"

I check La Verde's website. "Tickets on the British leg of this tour retail at £40."

"Fucking forty quid?" Craig says, spitting out some lager. "To be told how to get your fucking end away? Tell you what, Gaz, you've picked the right target here. I'm gonna take as much pleasure from making his audience eat shit as I am *him*. I suppose eighty quid for two tickets is a small price to pay."

"And you're sure the timers will work?"

"Well, no. I've only tested it a couple of times, and that was without a huge pile of faeces inside the devices. But there's fuck all else we can do to test it until we activate them. We'll just have to hope it does work, otherwise it's the best part of seven hundred quid wasted."

"What? Seven hundred quid?"

"Yeah, this equipment doesn't come cheap, you know. I had to order the timers from some company in America, and had to pay for express delivery to make sure they were here before this dickhead's next show. Then there's the Crapapults themselves, two of them for this instead of one. Then there's the tickets. It all adds up, you know."

"Right. I feel like I should contribute something but there's no way I can spend that much without Jenny noticing."

"I'll tell you one contribution you can make."

"What's that?"

"You can stop calling these Crapapults and call them Scatbombs."

"Why is that so important to you?"

"Coz that's a far more accurate description of what these actually do, for one thing."

"Is it?"

"Of course it fucking is. The other ones propelled the shit, these ones work completely differently. You know those cylinders they sometimes put in with the stolen loot when someone robs a bank? And they go off and cover them with compressed paint or dye or whatever? Well these are basically the same principle. Except they're a lot fucking bigger. So 'crapapult' doesn't really work. Besides, 'Operation Scatbomb' has a much better ring to it."

"Yeah," I agree reluctantly. "Fair enough. 'Operation Scatbomb' it is, then."

"Good lad," Craig says enthusiastically. "And as for not giving the game away to Jenny, well, you could always tell her about it, couldn't you?"

"Fucking hell, Clare Rayner, will you pack it in with the fucking relationship advice? I'm not being funny but, whatever fucking life-changing experiences you've been through, however your outlook on life has changed, you're still expecting me to take guidance from someone who rips off people's noses, shits through letterboxes or onto car seats, beats up coppers, calls himself 'Buckle' and has only ever actually been in a relationship of any kind for the amount of time it takes him to ejaculate into or onto the woman involved!"

"Oh, fuck off, Gaz. I've only ever ripped off one man's nose. One!"

"Well that's one more than the vast fucking majority of people!"

"Alright, fine," he shrugs, "keep massive secrets from her, I don't give a fuck that the guilt and shame will cause you to get a fucking ulcer, or that you're too fucking stupid to be able to keep secrets like that, so you'll somehow give yourself away and it'll damage or end your relationship. That's your fucking funeral, mate."

"Look, let's just focus on what we're meant to be doing for now, shall we? Let's concentrate on covering a crowd of micro-cocked sad sacks in faecal matter, and we'll finish this counselling session another time, okay? Anyway, I've got a fucking family therapy session to get to."

*

I'm really not in the mood for this shite today, and it seems the rest of my family aren't either. I'm amazed to see that Ben has actually turned up. After trying to punch me at the last session, I expected that to be his last appearance. As he is here, I decide to amuse myself by making a big show of attempting to give him a high-five. Of course, he "leaves me hanging", something I was relying on as I don't really wanna waste an antibacterial wipe on the chubby cunt.

"Gary, sit down, please." Kate gestures towards the remaining chair. She already seems annoyed with me, possibly due to my lateness, possibly due to my efforts to wind up my brother.

"Nice of you to join us," my dad chirps up. His arms are folded defensively across his chest.

"That's okay, Dad. I thought I'd give the three of you the chance to say all the stuff you're too fucking shithouse to say to my face."

"Shithouse? Who are you calling a shithouse?" Now it's Ben's turn to express himself without fear of judgement.

"You," I say, pointing at him. "Him," I add, pointing at Dad, "and her," pointing last of all at Mum.

"Alright, everyone," Kate interjects, later than I would have expected. "Can everyone just..."

She trails off. Seems like she's lost all her pep all of a sudden.

"What? Calm down?" I offer.

"Yes, can we just –"

"How am I expected to stay calm when my youngest son is constantly trying to provoke people? Me, my wife, my other son. I mean, I know he's a Tory bastard and everything –"

"Oi!" Ben shouts, suddenly stirring into life.

"He's got you there, Ben," I say.

"Your dad didn't mean it like that, Ben," Mum interrupts, trying harder than Kate seems to be to defuse things.

"Yes he did, Mum," I butt in. "Except he probably meant to say Tory cunt."

"Gary!" Suddenly Kate seems more alert, as though my use of that particular expletive has triggered some synapse in her brain.

"What, Kate? It's just a word. Besides which, he is one."

"Oh, fuck this shit."

Ben stands up and heads towards the door, ignoring Mum's appeals for him to stay.

"You're a fucking cunt an'all," he says, jabbing his finger at my face.

I shrug. "I don't recall ever saying otherwise. These all probably agree with you too." I gesture around the room, the looks of all present confirming this. "Don't let the door crush you on your way out, the missus' lawyer will be doing that soon enough."

Ben slams the door and my dad is looking at the floor, shaking his head.

"Is there any point in this? Any at all?" he says, looking up at Kate.

"Well..." she flounders.

I answer the question for her. "Probably not, really."

"I wouldn't say that, but certainly this week's session hasn't got off to a very good start. Perhaps we should draw things to an early conclusion. Give everyone time to process what's happened today."

"*Ha!*" I can't help but laugh. "Fine by me, but do you still get paid in full? Oh, what the fuck do I care? It's not me paying for these group sessions, it's these two gullible fuckers who are coughing up for it. If I were you two, though, I'd try and negotiate a reduced rate for this week."

I stand up and leave without another word as Dad shouts some lame insult I can't quite hear at my back.

*

I head back to the office, having taken nearly three hours for my lunch break, and tap on Eddie's door – a futile gesture because his door is, of course, always open, both literally and figuratively. In fact, I'm surprised he didn't have all the doors removed when the company moved in so as not to inhibit the free flow of ideas and energy or some such shit.

"Gary, hi. Come in."

"Eddie, I need to leave early today, if that's okay."

"Yeah, sure. No problem."

"I've got an... appointment."

Eddie looks back up from his computer, seemingly surprised that I'm offering any further explanation.

"Cool," he says.

I realise that, with Phil gone, and at least until another version of him is sent up, I've actually got a pretty easy life here. I may be surrounded by sandal-wearing male cleavage exposers but, as long as I don't fuck up too monumentally, I've got a job where I'm paid pretty well for doing very little real work, and am mostly left the fuck alone. I wonder why it has taken so long for this to occur to me.

"Eddie," I say. He looks back up, surprised that I'm still there.

"Yeah?"

"Erm... thanks."

"You're welcome, man. What for?"

"Oh, you know. Just... just thanks."

"Okay, man. You too."

*

"So, what's it for?"

"It's a tech conference."

"And they want you to go to it? Probably the least techy person in the company?"

"Well, yeah. It's tech *and* social media, so they thought it'd be best if I went."

I'm beginning to wish I'd taken more time to come up with a more believable story to explain my absence tonight to Jenny.

"And it's in Manchester?"

"That's right," I say, realising it may have been wiser to name a different city rather than the one where I plan to carry out the attack.

"Which venue?"

"It's at the erm... the Manchester Conference Centre."

"Never heard of it."

"I think it's a new one."

Jenny shrugs her shoulders. "Okay. Well, I suppose it's good that they want you to go, if completely perplexing. What time will you be back?"

"Not too late, probably by midnight."

"Okay, well have a good time, if that's possible at a tech conference. Sorry, a tech *and* social media conference."

"Will do, I'm gonna walk up to the main road and flag a taxi down."

*

I leave the flat and walk round the corner to where Craig is waiting, the engine of his van already running.

"Fucking come on, Gaz," he says as I climb in, "I've been waiting here for ages. What the fuck have you been doing?"

"Making a piss-poor attempt at explaining my absence tonight."

"Of course, the truth is always much easier to explain."

"For fuck's sake, will you just –"

"Yeah, yeah, just drop the whole 'tell her the truth' thing. Fine, you give yourself cancer from stress if you want, dickhead. See if I fucking care."

"Look, I know you mean well, I'm just having a bit of a hard time getting my head round this whole 'woke Buckle' thing."

"Whatever, dickhead. Come on," he says, putting the van into gear, "let's cover some pantie-sniffers in shit."

TWENTY-FOUR

Controversy surrounding Jonah La Verde's appearance in Manchester had already led to several venue changes as venues bowed to online pressure and cancelled his gig. This fucked with our initial plans, which had involved gaining access early on and planting our devices so that we could activate them by remote control. The initial location had an upper mezzanine which wouldn't have been in use and would have provided a perfect hiding spot. As it is, the third location, the only one willing to keep the booking in the face of online outrage, is a much smaller place, with no potential for stealth, so we've had to rethink.

Research tells us that, in an act of compromise aimed at placating protesters, the venue has refused to provide La Verde with any of its staff for the night, so security and ticketing will be taken care of by members of his own small entourage. This at least worked to our advantage, as our back-up plan was more akin to a ram-raid than the perfectly planned, almost militarily precise operation we'd first envisaged. A couple of professional bouncers would be unlikely to let a couple of guys carrying large bags into the event, but our thinking was that, in the worst case scenario, Craig would probably be able to kick the shit out of a couple of La Verde's Incel followers.

We park the van across the street just before eight o'clock. La Verde is due to hit the stage at half past, although "stage" is purely a figure of speech. The venue he has ended up at is a former Quaker meeting room, and our online research showed us that it still very much resembled one. The entrance area is little more than a small hallway leading into the main hall, which still appears to have the same floor the oat people would have once sat upon in silent contemplation, with a small raised platform at the front of the room giving the whole event the feel of a very misogynistic church raffle. We plan to sit in the van and wait until everyone is inside.

"Are you ready, then?" Craig says at about quarter to nine.

I nod my head whilst taking some very deep breaths.

"You sure? Can't having you fannying out on me at the last minute here, Gaz."

"No. I mean, yeah. I'm sure."

We get out of the van and walk around to the back doors. We take out the two Lonsdale holdalls and each sling one across our shoulders, Craig doing so with considerable more ease than I manage.

"Fuck," I say, wincing slightly. "They're heavy."

"Of course they're fucking heavy, they've got about a tonne of fucking faeces in them. Come on."

We cross the street. The main hall has a small window looking out onto the street. Through it, we can see La Verde in full swing. He's at the front of the room, walking back and forth along the front row of chairs. A quick scan of the room tells us there's only about forty people in there. "People" being a misnomer, as the audience is, of course, entirely comprised of men. Well, humans with the basic male genitalia, anyway. A venue this size, and he still can't fill it. Hardly the "voice of modern masculinity" that his website claims. Still, forty people listening to this waffle is forty too many.

"Right," Craig says quietly. "Let's fucking do this prick."

We approach the main entrance and, as expected, we are greeted by two tired-looking members of La Verde's "staff" performing security and ticketing duties. Given his clientele, it was presumably assumed that two skinny fuckers with glasses and shit alt-right haircuts would be sufficient security. Most nights, that would probably be correct.

"Oh, hey, guys," one of them seated at the reception desk says, smiling through his tiredness. The other guy, standing behind him, eyes us suspiciously. "Erm, the talk has already started."

"That's okay," Craig says, "we've seen him before, he always peaks around the middle of the night anyway. You know, really brings his bitch-hating A-Game."

"Huh-huh, yeah," the dweeb laughs uncertainly. "You got your tickets?"

"Yeah. Give him the tickets, Lance," Craig says to me. I'm suddenly frozen to the spot, though, and my brain's commands to my hands to pass the tickets over go unheard.

"Lance! Give him the fucking tickets."

I manage to hand them over with a sweaty, shaking hand. The first yank checks them and places them in the box. We begin to walk towards the main hall.

"Yo, what's in the bags, guys?" The second prick has now piped up.

"What, these? Oh nothing much, just Lance's spare trousers. He pisses himself and ejaculates uncontrollably if he ever sees a woman, so we have to take these everywhere we go. Not that there's much chance of seeing any women at one of these gigs, of course, but one of them might be getting picked up by their mum, and one look at her would be enough to set him off. Come on, Lance, let's go see Jonah."

"Hang on a minute, fellas," the second guy continues, trying to adopt a vaguely tough voice and stance. "I'm gonna need to see what you've got in there, okay?"

Again I'm frozen and unable to respond. Fortunately, Craig is happy to take a lead here.

"Actually, Brad or Chad or whatever your fucking name is. It's not okay. This is our personal property. We've paid for tickets to come and worship at the altar of Jonah La Verde, one of the great, free-thinking virgins of our time, and that's what we intend to do, okay?"

Suddenly feeling inappropriately emboldened, the second dweeb steps out from behind the desk, the friendlier first guy now visibly shaking with the tension.

"Look, if you don't show me what's in the bag, you're gonna have to leave, okay?"

"Actually, neither of those things are gonna be happening," Craig says as he hands the second bag over to me. "Best thing you can do is probably just go back to supporting that wall over there and let us in to see our hero."

"Look guys, can everyone just, like, calm down a little, yeah?" the first guy chirps up nervously, but his associate is now at that particular point some men reach where, having taken a stand, to back down now would seem like the ultimate act of cowardice, and he has no choice but to continue along this badly-chosen route.

"What's your name, buddy?" he asks Craig.

"Buddy?" Craig says, stepping towards the pair of them. "No, me name's not Buddy. IT'S FUCKING BUCKLE!"

He reaches over the desk, grabs the first lad by his swept over hair, and slams his face hard into the desk, knocking him out instantly. The second dweeb's tough-guy act drops as quickly as his arsehole presumably does, and he lets out a little yelp.

"What the... what the fuck, buddy?"

"BUCKLE!"

Craig runs towards him and smashes his forehead into his face.

"Get in there and get it done, Gaz," he says, turning to me. "I'll keep an eye on these two."

I run into the hall, where La Verde is standing in the middle of the centre aisle, both he and the audience already looking towards me, our commotion having presumably disrupted his talk.

"What the hell is going on out there?" La Verde says, his anger quickly turning to alarm as he sees the bags in my hand. "What is this? What's happening?"

His alarm is no doubt only increased by the fact that I'm so nervous I can't speak. Instead, I stand there shaking, sweating and holding two large bags which, for all he knows, could contain anything. What seems like minutes pass by as me and La Verde stand and stare, his mini army of unfuckables watching on. The eerie silence is broken only by Craig pushing the door open and joining me.

"What the fuck, Ga-Lance? What are you fucking waiting for?"

"Waiting for? Waiting to do what?" La Verde is now visibly terrified.

Craig takes a step towards him and points a finger at his face.

"SHIT T.J. MACKIE!" he chants. "YOU'RE JUST A SHIT T.J. MACKIE!"

He takes the bags from me, dumps them on the floor and unzips them.

"I wouldn't move if I was you, Jonah, lad," he says.

La Verde stays frozen to the spot in terror, as does everyone else. We back out of the door and close it, Craig locking it with a key he presumably liberated from one of the guys who are now writhing around on the floor in a state of semi-consciousness. He takes the timer out of his pocket and presses the button. We hear two loud popping noises, followed instantly by anguished cries.

"Oh my God!"

"What the fuck? WHAT THE FUCK?"

"IT'S SHIT! IT'S ACTUALLY FUCKING SHIT!"

"Sounds like the remote worked," I say.

He nods his head, takes an *Operation Scatbomb* card out of his pocket, and throws it onto the floor.

"You two really need to get yourselves girlfriends," he says as we step over them.

TWENTY-FIVE

"That got a bit messy, didn't it?" I say as we head back along the motorway.

"Messy? It was Operation Scatbomb, of course it got fucking messy."

"I mean, you know, the head butting and that. That wasn't really expected, was it?"

"Listen, Gaz. You've willingly engaged in two acts involving the covering of strangers in shit. If the thing that stands out to you in that is a bit of low-level physical violence, you wanna have a word with yourself, mate."

"Yeah. They deserved it anyway, right?"

"For fuck's sake, Gaz. It's a bit fucking late to be getting an attack of fucking conscience now, mate. You wanna drive back and fucking apologise to them or something? Maybe help the fuckers clean the shit out of their fucking side partings?"

"No! I dunno. It's just... fuck 'em, you're right."

"Look, inasmuch as anyone anywhere deserves to have shit exploded all over them, then yeah, they fucking did. But if you're gonna have a wrestle with your inner fucking voice or whatever, then the only sane fucking response is no, they didn't fucking deserve it. But we're a bit fucking past that now, aren't we?"

We finish the rest of the journey in near silence. Craig eventually drops me off around the corner from the flat.

"Listen," he says as I'm getting out of the van, "when you've finished working through whatever fucking internal conflict you're having about this, come round and see me, and we can plan the next one. Or we can leave it. Whatever. All I'll say is that the last week or so is the happiest I've ever seen you. Or the least fucking miserable I've ever seen you, anyway."

*

Jenny is lying on the couch when I get in, watching something on Netflix. I don't know what it is but it has an English actor I vaguely recognise doing a shit American accent. She pauses it when I come in.

"Alright?" she says.

"Yeah."

"How did the conference go?"

"Oh, you know. How you'd expect. Lots of people talking about stuff."

"Bit conferency, then?"

I shrug my shoulders. Jenny resumes the drama she's watching, and I get a flash of Jonah La Verde's face as he looked at the bags and one of the gobby little fucker on the door when he shat it at the sight of his mate being Buckled.

"What are you smiling at?" Jenny says.

"What? Oh, nothing." And I hear the sound of screaming from inside the hall as the scat-bombs were activated. "How long of this is left?"

"About twenty minutes. Why?"

"I'm gonna go and have a quickish shower, then. See you in there?"

Jenny gives a little grin of her own. "Yeah, okay."

*

The next morning I'm out of the flat five minutes earlier than was my routine to allow myself a small detour to buy my morning coffee from an establishment I've been frequenting of late, for obvious reasons. Before I reach work, I stop outside Bean Grinder – still lifeless, though much cleaner looking than it was. A sign is taped up on the inside of the front window. *"Closed until further notice. Thanks for your solidarity",* it says.

I squint through the window and I think I see a lonely looking figure in the back, shuffling around like a Scottish widow. I decide that, given the proximity of my barring and the subsequent attack, it might be best if I wasn't seen in the vicinity of Bean Grinder for a while, so I continue into work.

When I get there, Eddie is standing at the top of the stairs, actually fucking high-fiving people as they arrive. There's some loud pop music that I don't recognise playing in the background.

"Hey, Gary," he says, considerately offering me a less unhygienic fist bump instead. I shake my head but accept that there is at least some temporary cause for celebration, with Phil out of the way, so allow my knuckles to lightly brush against his.

"There's pastries, doughnuts and coffee for everyone, dude. Help yourself."

I gesture towards my coffee.

"Oh," he says, "well go and grab some pastries, anyway."

"Nah, I'm okay, thanks, Eddie. I think I'm just gonna get to work."

"Oh come on, man," he says, with an enthusiasm that suggests he's started early on the coke this morning. "Just come and hang with us for ten minutes, grab a doughnut or something."

He seems so genuinely hurt at the prospect of my refusing his hospitality that I relent and wander into the main office, where people are stuffing their faces. People turn and nod at me, a couple of *"hey, Gary"* greetings making their way past chewed-up pastry. I pick up some sort of elaborate thing with swirling icing and pecans on it and take a bite, and sip at my coffee. Pretty much the entire company is gathered together and I'm sure that I haven't seen at least a quarter of them before, let alone have any idea what their jobs are. I see a few glance in my direction, no doubt thinking the same thing, and hope that none of them ask me what I actually do here. They're all young, talented, good-looking and vibrant people, and standing here among so many of them highlights more than ever what an ungrateful fraud I am. I decide I need to get out of there before anyone approaches me and asks me if this is my first day.

"Have a good day, Gary," I hear someone say as I attempt to leave stealthily.

"Have a good day, everyone," I say without fully turning my head.

It's embarrassingly half-hearted but is still the friendliest thing I've said or done in all the time I've worked here.

TWENTY-SIX

Benjamin hasn't made it to this week's family therapy session. I'm partly glad because it means I don't have to look at his ever-widening face, and partly disappointed that I can't make this session more bearable by winding the fucker up.

"He had to be somewhere else," my mum says to Kate by way of explanation. "Somewhere very important. Oh, not that this isn't important, of course."

"That's fine, Janet, nobody is obliged to come here. If I may ask, though, where was it he had to be? If that's not too intrusive a question," Kate asks, smelling bullshit, I think.

"Well, he and his wife are trying to work through their difficulties. I think they're having some sort of relationship counselling."

I can't help but let out a huge laugh.

"Don't laugh at your mother, Gary," Dad chirps up.

"Alright, take it easy, Prince Valiant."

"Don't get smart-mouthed with me, lad."

Again, I can't help but laugh.

"'Lad'? Have you been watching some Jimmy McGovern shows or something, Dad? What's with the sudden scouse hard-man act?"

"Look," he says, leaning forward in his chair. "I just won't have you laughing at your mother. Or me. Not anymore. I've had enough of it."

"Paul, Gary. Let's just take a moment, shall we?" Kate attempts to cool the already high levels of tension in the room.

"You see the aggression in his voice and body language, Kate? For the second time in these sessions of so-called mediation, I'm being physically threatened by members of my immediate family. And all because I couldn't help but let out a little fucking chortle at the ludicrous suggestion that my brother and his wife are sitting somewhere together trying to work things out instead of where we all know they really are. Which is at a meeting with their solicitors, where Benjamin will find out exactly the extent to which his gold-digging cunt of a wife is gonna ream the arse out of his fucking finances."

"Gary!" Mum bursts into tears.

"For fuck's sake, Gary!" Dad shouts.

"Gary, that really isn't at all helpful." Kate doesn't quite shout but it's pretty fucking close.

"For fuck's sake, what? Not fucking helpful why? I thought we were meant to be honest in here. With ourselves and each other. How fucking honest is it to sit here and blatantly fucking lie, or completely delude ourselves, about the reality right in front of us? Mum, you may not want to hear this but Ben's family is falling apart. It's fucked, just as yours has been for many, many years now. That doesn't necessarily reflect badly on you, or Dad. It's just what fucking happens sometimes. Especially to pricks like Ben!"

"Gary, please, just –" Kate attempts to interrupt me.

"Just what, Kate? Just participate in this ridiculous fucking charade? What the fuck is wrong with this family? Why can't we just accept what a mess we are, either individually or collectively? It's fucking weird! Mum, what are you gonna tell the neighbours when he has to move back in because his wife has left him homeless? That he's visiting while he has another happiness wing built onto his fucking house?"

"WILL YOU FUCKING SHUT UP?!" Dad shouts, abandoning his post as Mum's comforter in chief and standing up in front of me.

I stand up to face him.

"I MIGHT DO IF YOU STOP ACTING LIKE CHARLES FUCKING BRONSON ALL OF A FUCKING SUDDEN!"

I look down and see his fist clenching. Oh, this is just *too* promising a fucking prospect.

"Paul, maybe you should sit down," Kate says very quietly. But I can tell she's as curious as I am to see where this goes. I'm sure she'd never admit it, but her anthropological curiosity has now far overtaken her professional decorum. She wants to see what will happen, and she knows full well that, whatever does happen, I absolutely fucking deserve it.

"I'd stand back if I was you, Kate. It seems Max Farnham is about to go rogue. You gonna hit me, Dad?"

"I'm not sure. Maybe."

Mum has now stopped crying quite so hysterically and is just sobbing lightly as she too watches the events unfold, like someone who's somehow wandered into the middle of a dog fight in a country barn and is disgusted but curious in equal measure.

I move a step closer to Dad. I lean my chin right into his face and tap it with my index finger a few times. "Go on, Dad," I say, "have a fucking pop. We all know you want to. We all know I probably fucking deserve it too. Nobody's gonna think any worse of you for it. In fact, maybe this is where you two have been going wrong all these years. Maybe a few good beatings would have sorted me and Ben out a bit. Maybe your liberal parenting has always been the issue and you should have just given in to your primal urges and just... fucking... chinned us both."

Kate isn't even attempting to intervene now. She's just watching with utter fascination. As is Mum.

"I won't press any charges or anything. And even if I did, five minutes with any judge talking to me and they're bound to let you off."

His mouth is tightening, short, nervous breaths coming from his nose. His fist clenches more.

"You absolute horrible bastard," he says quietly.

And of course, he's right. It must be hard being a parent, I suppose. One day, your kids are looking up at you adoringly from their cot, totally dependent on and in awe of you. The next day, you're finding wank rags under their bed. Then, before you know it, they're shoving you into an old folks' home where you're left to wallow in your own bodily fluids and be beaten by underpaid "care" staff, while they wait for you to cark it so they can claim their inheritance. And in some cases, before the nursing home stage, they might even be standing in front of you in a counselling session trying to goad you into physically assaulting them.

"Well?" I say, jutting my chin out an inch more.

My chin, however, remains untouched as Dad surprises me with a punch to the guts. I go down instantly, winded.

"Paul!" Mum says, but it's less of an admonishment, than a *"my hero"* expression of surprise and admiration.

"Fuck. I'm sorry, Gary," he says, trying to help me up. I push his hand away and he makes no further attempt. He goes to his chair and gets his jacket.

Kate stands. "I think we've probably taken these sessions as far as they can go," she says to my parents.

They nod in agreement and leave without looking back at me.

Kate walks over to me and crouches down as I attempt to suck some air back into my lungs.

"I think it's probably best if you find yourself another therapist from now on, Gary."

I nod in agreement, and struggle to my feet and towards the door.

"Oh, Gary?" Kate says just before I close it. "This session's on the house."

TWENTY-SEVEN

Jenny switches on the radio as she steps out of the shower and into the bedroom. Laying her clothes out on the bed, she's only half listening to regional news reports as she plugs in her hairdryer.

"In the second such incident in the region in as many weeks, a public appearance by controversial Canadian author and self-styled pick-up artist Jonah La Verde was disrupted by what police are describing as a 'dirty attack', involving the use of human excrement –"

Jenny switches her hairdryer on, then instantly switches it back off upon hearing the word "excrement".

"… talk in Manchester. Reports say two men forced their way into the meeting, assaulting two people and locking attendees inside before setting off some kind of explosive device filled with faeces…"

Her heart nearly stops when she hears the location of the attack. She drops her hairdryer to the floor and runs to the bed and types "Manchester excrement attack" into her smartphone. Clicking on the first of several reports, she looks for the date of the attack, which she had missed on the radio. It confirms what she already instinctively knew. It was last night, while Gary was in Manchester. She Googles the first attack on the coffee shop and checks the location. It was barely a hundred yards from his office.

"Fucking hell, Gary," she says aloud. "What the fucking hell have you been up to?"

She goes into her phone's contacts and dials her boss's direct extension number.

"Hi, Karen, it's Jenny. Sorry, but I won't be coming in today. I've... got the shits."

TWENTY-EIGHT

"What about a police station?" Craig asks, unwrapping his sandwich as I hold the door of the café open for him.

"Fuck no. Didn't you read the article?" I say, shoving my phone under his nose as we walk, the link to the online article I found still open. "I think the last thing we need to be doing at this point is antagonising the police. It says here they're looking for us. They know the incidents are linked –"

"What? You're fucking joking?! You mean they've figured out that two essentially identical attacks in the same region within the space of a few days might be the work of the same people? Shit a brick, they must have their best detectives working on the case. They're onto us, Gaz. We'd best just go and hand ourselves in, eh? Maybe cop a plea bargain or something? Or I could just rat you out, anything to save myself, I mean, the fucking net is closing in after all, right?"

"Oh, fuck off."

"Nah, I get your point, even if it was made in a fucking ridiculously idiotic way. Plod aren't necessarily our kind of targets anyway. Fox hunters?"

"I dunno," I shrug. "I mean, they're obviously scum but they're riding horses all over the place, so it'd be pretty hard logistically to plan. Plus some of those fuckers carry shotguns and stuff."

"Oh, fucking hell, yeah," Craig agrees. "Fucking country cunts."

We reach Craig's studio building and he lets us in. We walk up the stairs and sit down either side of his desk as he eats his sandwich.

"Well fucking who, then?" he says.

"I don't fucking know... I'm thinking."

His buzzer sounds loudly, actually making him drop his sandwich.

"Who the fuck is that?" I ask.

"How the fuck should I know?"

Neither of us says it, but I know the same thought has occurred to us both. Have the police already caught up with us? Did Craig leave traces of his DNA embedded in the face of one of the fellas he twatted unconscious in Manchester? Has circumstantial evidence identified me as a suspect for the Bean Grinder? Do they plan to sweat me down in an interrogation room, or simply beat a confession out of me like in the good old days?

"Are you gonna answer it, Craig?"

"No, of course not. I'm gonna just ignore it while you shit yourself in fear."

"Oh, like it hasn't crossed your fucking mind that that buzz is the prelude to the door getting smashed off its hinges and us getting pepper-sprayed to fuck before we get thrown into the back of a police van."

"What the fuck are you on about, you daft twat? It's not the fucking police, Gary. There's no fucking way. There's just no fucking way."

"Well go and answer it, then, if you're so fucking confident."

"Alright, I will answer it. See if I give a fuck. It's not like I've never been thrown in the back of a police van before," he says, approaching the intercom. He turns back before he reaches it. "But it's not the fucking police, alright?"

He sounds emphatic but I know he's trying to convince himself as much as me. He picks up the handset.

"Hello? Erm, yeah?" He looks back over at me, the confidence suddenly gone from his eyes. "Oh right. You'd better come in, then."

He replaces the handset.

"Well? Who the fuck is it?" I ask. "The police?"

"No. It's worse than that. For you, anyway."

"What? Why? Who is it?"

"It's Jenny."

I feel my internal organs collide somewhere around my rectum.

"Oh," I say.

TWENTY-NINE

"Jenny, what the fuck are you doing here?" I ask as she enters the studio looking around warily. "How did you even know where to find me?"

"I followed you."

"What? You fucking followed me? Are you serious? Why the fuck would you do that?"

"Yeah, it's pretty shady and duplicitous, isn't it? But, given your recent activities, I'd say that still currently leaves me with the moral fucking high ground, wouldn't you?"

Craig is watching the conversation bounce back and forth like someone watching a game of table tennis, but a game of table tennis where one participant might be about to kick the shit out of the other.

"What do you mean?" I say.

Jenny looks over at Craig. "Well, as he's clearly too fucking ignorant to introduce us, I suppose I'll have to introduce myself. I take it you're Craig."

"That's me. People call me Buckle, though. Except for this cunt, that is."

"Right," Jenny says, cautiously offering him a hand to shake. "I think I'll stick with Craig. Nice to meet you. I think. I've heard lots about you."

"Likewise, it's a fucking pleasure."

Jenny turns back to me. "Now, are you gonna tell me what the fuck you've been up to, Gary?"

"What? Why am I the one being interrogated? I'm not the one that's behaving like a fucking Le Carré character. Have you bugged my phones too?"

"Of course I haven't, that'd mean bugging my own fucking phones, Gary. Which doesn't make any sense. A bit like your recent activities."

"I don't know what you're talking about," I protest, not remotely convincingly.

"For fuck's sake, Gary. Am I a fucking idiot? Is that really gonna be your response to this? Is *that* how you wanna deal with this?"

I look over at Craig, who has finished his sandwich and opened a can of beer. He shrugs his shoulders.

"Just fucking tell her," he says. "Do what I've been telling you to do and just fucking tell her."

"Alright. Jenny, you might wanna sit down."

*

Craig takes himself off into a corner. Jenny sits, and I make my second major confession of recent times to her. I tell her everything we've have been up to, omitting no detail. I tell her how and why I chose the targets; Craig occasionally wanders over and fills in the gaps on the technicalities of the scat-bombs; I tell her about him breaking the faces of the two Canadian cunts at the La Verde gig.

"Hang on." Jenny stops me when she's figured out the precise chronology. "That night you came back to the flat a bit early, and... you know... the kitchen. That was...?"

"After the coffee shop attack, yeah."

"Fucking hell, Gary. That's the weirdest fucking aphrodisiac I've ever heard of."

I hear a snort of laughter from Craig and tell him to fuck off.

"So, what's next?" Jenny continues. "I mean, is that it, are you planning more of these things?"

I look sheepishly over at Craig, who just shrugs again.

"We were thinking of it, yeah."

"On who, exactly?"

"Well, we haven't really figured it out yet," I say. "That's what we've been talking about today."

Jenny stands up and paces around the room. Once more I'm convinced that this is it, that things are over. And who could fucking blame her? She's put up with a lot in our time together but knowing her boyfriend is a scat-bomb terrorist is more than even the most tolerant of people are likely to be able to take. She walks back over to me.

"I think I've got an idea," she says.

"What?"

Craig walks over to us. "An idea?" he says.

"Yeah. For your next... attack. Target. Whatever. I know who you can hit."

"Jenny..." I begin, but have nothing else.

"What? What's the problem? You've told me everything now so you've nothing to hide from me anymore. I've got an idea and I think you'll like it."

I look over at Craig.

"Fine by me," he says.

Jenny turns to him. "Got any more of those cans?"

THIRTY

"Have you ever heard of White Action?"

Jenny is sat down with me and Craig, spelling out her idea for us.

"No," I say, "but I imagine it's either some shit indie band or a far-right group."

"The latter. Proper fucking neo-Nazi scum, they are. And they're coming *here.*"

"Didn't the last few loads of Nazis basically get chased into the lost luggage at Lime Street then straight out of the city?"

"Yeah, which means either they'll come with a lot more this time, looking for revenge, or there'll be so few of them that they'd be an easy target."

"When?" Craig asks.

"When what?"

"When are these fuckers coming?"

Jenny takes out her phone and does a quick search. "The seventeenth," she says.

"That's just over a week away," I point out. "Not very long to plan it."

"Long enough if we get to work now," Craig counters. "What do you think, Gaz? Ideal target, surely."

"Perfect," I agree. "No question. I just don't know if it's time enough. It'll be a lot harder than the last two."

"Why?" says Jenny.

"Moving targets," Craig says. "The other two were in a confined space. We just had to go into where they were. Not even that, the first time around. These Combat 18 types will be on the move though, right? On a march, is it?"

Jenny nods.

"There's bound to be a heavy police presence too," I say. "There always is for this kind of shit, but after the last couple of times it's bound to be even heavier."

Craig nods. "This is tricky. The target is harder and the pigs being there'll make things even more complicated. Before, we just had to make sure we gave it toes before the police came. This time, they'll be there already. In numbers. It'll require a change of tactics, no fucking doubt."

He leans back in his chair and closes his eyes for a moment, apparently lost in thought, or possibly just having an untimely nap. Jenny and I look at each other, wondering what we should do next.

Suddenly, Craig leaps up and runs to his desk and begins typing furiously at his keyboard.

"Are you sure about this, Jenny?" I ask quietly.

She comes and sits next to me. "I don't know. I mean, were *you* when you first decided to do it?"

"Fuck, no! It's madness, isn't it? I still can't believe we ever did it. I can't believe we drove to Manchester to do it a second time. And I certainly can't believe we're contemplating doing it for a third time, and that you're now involved."

"I can't believe you ever did it. But, now you have, I don't think it's that much of a leap for me to want to be involved. The situation itself is ridiculous enough that me joining you doesn't really make much difference. Does it? Are you okay with me being involved?"

"Yeah, I think I am. Plus, this way I can claim it as credits towards actually socialising with you, can't I?"

Jenny laughs. "Well, attacking Nazis with poo wasn't what I had in mind. I was thinking, more, dinner with friends."

"But?"

"But, in the absence of anything else..."

"Right, you two," Craig shouts from his desk. "I think I've got it. I've fucking got it. Come and have a look at this."

We walk over to his desk and he tilts his computer monitor towards us to show us what he's been looking at.

"Well?" he asks. "What do you think?"

"Oh, wow," Jenny says.

"That might work, Craig. That might just fucking work," I say.

My phone vibrates loudly in my pocket. I take it out and see that it's my mum calling.

"Who is it?" Jenny says.

"Mum," I reply, ignoring the call and putting the phone back into my pocket.

"Aren't you gonna answer it?"

"Not really a good time, Jenny."

"Gary!"

Jenny's phone now begins to ring loudly and she takes it out and answers it.

"Hi, Janet," she says, glaring at me as she walks towards another corner of the studio.

"Well, this is a turn up for the fucking books, isn't it, Gary?" Craig says when she's wandered off.

"Just a bit, like."

"She doesn't look too happy now, mind," Craig says as Jenny walks back over.

He's right. She doesn't look happy at all.

"What's up?" I ask.

"It's your dad, Gary. He's had a stroke."

"For fuck's sake."

THIRTY-ONE

By the time we get to Arrowe Park hospital Dad has passed through A&E and is now convalescing on a ward. Jenny and I take the lift up to the third floor and follow a few signs around looking for the correct ward. As we find it, we approach the nurses station to ask which bed he's in when I hear my mum calling me.

I look up and she's walking towards us, make-up smudged and running from her tears.

"Oh, Gary," she says, putting her arms round me.

"Fuck, he's not dead, is he?"

"What? No. He's over there. Bed five. He's very tired."

"Maybe we should leave him alone, then."

"No, he said he wants to see you when you get here."

"Right, so he can speak?"

"Yes, he's just slurring a bit, and a bit slow."

"How bad is it, Mum?"

"Well, Gary, why don't you go and speak to your father and see for yourself?"

I look at Jenny, who nods encouragement. "Okay," I say, and walk over towards bed five.

Dad is lying back, propped up by a few pillows, with his eyes closed. I sit in the hard plastic chair at the side of his bed. The chair squeaks as I drag it closer, and Dad opens his eyes and sees me.

"Alright, Dad?"

He nods his head weakly.

"What happened?" I ask.

His lips move in an odd way, like he's trying to close them around the reed of an invisible oboe. "In garden centre... face felt numb... didn't know where we were."

"You know where you are now?"

He nods. "Garden centre."

"No, Dad. You're not in the garden centre now, you're in—"

"Joking," he says quietly.

"Oh, right. Good one. So it can't have been *too* serious."

He shakes his head. "Felt serious."

"Yeah, I bet. Must have been a bit fucking scary. For Mum too."

He nods.

"Look, Dad –"

"Sorry."

"Sorry? Sorry for what, Dad?"

"Lots. Must have got lots of things wrong."

"No, it's not as simple as –"

"Shouldn't have hit you. Sorry."

"Oh, fuck that. I've had it coming for thirty years, Dad. Everybody knows that. Don't worry about it."

I can see some tears coming from his eyes and rolling down the side of his face past his ear.

"Dad, it's okay. You'll be alright."

He turns his head to me. "L... love you, Gary. Me... Jan... love you. Sorry if we've let you down. If we... failed you."

He struggles with the *f* sound in "failed", and it comes out more like *"pwailed"*. I put my hand on his wrist and squeeze it gently.

"Dad, you don't have to apologise. It is what it is. You may have made some mistakes, but I don't think it really would have made much difference. The way I am, it's not just down to you. I'm just a fucking anomaly."

I tell him to rest and walk back over to Mum and Jenny, who have been standing by the mains doors watching me.

"He's gonna have a rest now," I say to Mum. She nods and wipes her eyes.

"I'm glad you came."

"Sorry for ignoring your call. If I'd known..."

"That's alright. You two can go home now, I'll ring you if there's any change."

Mum moves in for a hug and, after a brief hesitation, I allow it, and even hug her back. Just a bit.

We leave the ward and head towards the lift just as Ben steps out of it. I stop when I see him but realise there's nowhere to go to avoid him. He looks around at the signs on the wall before he spots me and, having also apparently realised there's no way to the ward other than past me, slowly walks towards me. Jenny walks on ahead of me, giving him the slightest of hellos before he reaches me.

"Have you seen him?" Ben says.

I nod.

"How is he?"

I consider lying. Exaggerating Dad's condition, just to fuck with him. But I think better of it.

"Not too bad. He's weak, he's tired. He's slurring some words a bit. But, considering he had a stroke a few hours ago, he's not too bad."

"Right. Good. I didn't bring any grapes or anything. Did you? Is that something people actually do?"

"I don't know. I didn't. I don't think it's really an issue, to be honest."

"No," he says, nodding. "Gary?"

"What?"

"We've both been awful sons, haven't we?"

"Yeah, pretty much."

"Maybe we can try to a bit better from now on?"

"I don't know. Maybe."

"Right. Well I'd better get in there."

Ben walks into the ward and I walk towards the lift, where Jenny is waiting for me.

THIRTY-TWO

The three of us are squeezed into the front of Craig's van, which is parked at the corner of Copperas Hill and Skelhorne Street, just around the corner from Lime Street. We're on double yellow lines and I'm feeling conspicuous and so nervous my cock and balls have shrivelled to the size of a baby carrot and two chick peas.

"Can't we just park a bit further away?" I say. "I mean, any passing copper is gonna at least tell us to move and probably wanna search the van. We're asking for trouble here."

"Look, I fucking told you. We can't park any further away than this. Even this is pushing it. The less distance the carts have to travel, the better. We're just gonna have to take a chance with being parked here."

Jenny nods in agreement. "I'm fucking bricking it too, Gary. But I don't think we can move any further than this."

I know they're right, but that doesn't stop my arsehole twitching. "What's the time?"

"Fucking two minutes since you last asked me, Gaz. Fucking relax. Or at least try and be a bit less fucking anxious, will you?"

"Right, sorry. And what time are the main lot all due in?"

"FUCKING HALF EIGHT! THE FUCKING TIME HASN'T FUCKING CHANGED, GARY. WE'VE BEEN OVER THE PLAN! NOT ONE FUCKING THING HAS CHANGED, ALRIGHT? NOW FUCKING PACK IT IN!"

Jenny puts a reassuring hand on my arm. "There's no need to fucking yell at him," she says quietly but emphatically to Craig. "He's only fucking asking. There's no harm in going over the plans again, is there?"

I realise how lucky and bizarre it is that I have a girlfriend not only willing to join me in attacking some pretty violent neo-Nazis but to stand up to Buckle on my behalf.

"Yeah, alright, Xena Warrior Princess. Like the old saying goes: 'Fail to prepare, prepare to have three scat-bombs backfire on you'."

The plan, such as it is, has a lot more potential for failure than our first two attacks. We knew there was fuck all chance of us getting close enough to White Action without either getting kicked half to death by them or getting arrested by the police. Quite possibly both.

We'd managed to glean that the bulk of the group would be arriving at Lime Street at half eight, with another train carrying a few members arriving just minutes later. These two groups would be met on the concourse by a group of "activists" before beginning their march at nine o'clock. Various right-wing groups had boasted on Twitter that hundreds were expected. In truth, only a few dozen were likely to show, and they were likely to be far outnumbered by both police and anti-fascist protesters.

The police had grudgingly allowed the group to march from the steps of Lime Street down only as far as the top of

Renshaw Street, where they would then turn around and head back to where they started. The walk would take a normal person a matter of minutes, but with the shuffling, simian gait common to most fascists it'll probably take them several times that. Not that they'll ever get close to finishing their march, if our plan works out.

THIRTY-THREE

Craig checks the time for approximately the fiftieth time in five minutes. Clearly, his nerves are almost as frayed as mine.

"Alright," he says, "it's three minutes to nine. Let's get started."

Jenny and I nod slowly. "Okay," we say.

We get out of the van and walk round to the back door. We all check over our shoulders one last time. Craig opens the doors, leans in and takes out the first cart, placing it carefully down on the road. A remote-controlled, three-wheeled golf cart, purchased online. But, instead of having a golf bag attached to it, this one carries a scat-bomb identical to the ones we used in Manchester, which fits snugly into the holster usually occupied by a set of clubs. The carts cost just under two hundred pounds each, which, added to the cost of the devices themselves, made this by far our most expensive venture yet. This time, with no need to keep our actions hidden from Jenny, the cost was at least shared between the three of us. Inside the van are two more carts, carrying the exact same payload. Jenny lifts down the second cart and I lift down the third.

We line them up next to each other at the top of Skelhorne Street. Usually this street would be lined with taxis waiting to pick commuters up from the station. No doubt anticipating the chaos today's march would cause, though, all the cabbies have decided to position themselves elsewhere.

"Okay, disguises on," Craig instructs.

With this likely to be our most high-profile act yet, Craig insisted on more elaborate disguises than hoodies. As well as replacing his van registration plates with false ones, he has also ordered three masks. When we opened the box they were delivered in, Jenny and I were stunned to see the face of Ainsley Harriott staring out at us.

"Why Ainsley Harriott?" I'd asked.

"Because, if any of these cunts actually see us, imagine how much more humiliating it'll be for them to have been had by a famous black poofter."

"He's not gay, though, is he?"

"Who cares? Most people think he is, and I bet those Nazi twats do too," Craig said.

"Fair enough," Jenny had said, trying her mask on.

By the time we have our carts in position, it is just seconds from nine. We pull our masks on over our faces and sit on the back of the van. Craig takes out his laptop, Jenny her phone, and I take out my tablet. In an act I couldn't help but be hugely impressed by, Craig has linked the remote control for each cart to one of these devices and installed a small webcam to the carts. This way, we can control the progress of our individual cart and guide it via the camera, reducing the need for us to be close to the incident and reducing the risk of us being caught. When I complimented him on his ingenuity he shrugged it off as though it was a mere bagatelle, which it now was to him.

In the midst of the frenzied activity since he kidnapped me, it had somehow failed to register with me just what a smart fucker Craig had revealed himself to have become. Still utterly fucking psychotic, of course. But smart too.

We all begin to slowly direct the carts down the hill towards Lime Street. The growing noise tells us we were probably about right with our timing. We can hear loud chanting, though it's impossible to tell whether it is the marchers or the protesters. We know that the protesters have, fortunately enough, been positioned by the police outside St George's Hall. Although some are bound to break through police lines and risk being caught in the line of fire, most should be safe, and have a great view. And any that do get caught up in the event will simply be collateral damage. They won't be hurt – not by us, anyway – and I'm sure there's one or two amongst the Antifa crowd who'd thoroughly deserve a good splattering.

We watch our unsteady progress on our respective devices as we trundle downhill. My cart accidentally bumps up against one of the others and then against the kerb and I think it's going to topple over and that I'll let Jenny and Craig down, but somehow it manages to defy gravity and continue its slow progress.

Through the mounted cameras, we see White Action slowly coming into view along Lime Street. As expected, there's barely twenty of them, and they are making slow, pathetic progress along the street. There's no sound on our cameras but we can see that even their chanting is half-hearted and is so quiet we can't hear them from barely two hundred yards away.

I worry that, despite their Walking Dead-esque meandering, we may have started our descent too late and risked missing them, but the slight downward slope of the street speeds us up and we end up having to brake to stop the carts rolling past them. We turn each cart towards them and see the few Nazis in their balaclavas and half-face masks stop and look nervously into the cameras. One of them steps towards mine and peers down at it. He points at it and I lip-read him saying *"What the fuck's this?"* Another shite supremacist leans into Jenny's, and a few more gather over their shoulders while the rest hang back nervously.

"Get ready," Craig says. "Right, one... two... three... GO!"

We all press the appropriate buttons. We hear a faint distant popping sound, and on the cameras everything goes brown.

THIRTY-THREE

For the first time, we can clearly hear the scum as they scream as one. Even louder is the laughter of the protesters, who until now had remained silent, no doubt not deeming this pathetic trickle of Nazis even worth fully protesting against.

"Got you, you cunts!" Craig shouts.

We hear screams, initially distant but getting closer. Looking up, we see a single Nazi fleeing the scene, shit all over his legs and fat gut. Craig places his laptop down and steps slowly towards the top of the road. As the fleeing Nazi draws almost level with us, Craig sprints towards him, jumps into the air and delivers a crunching roundhouse kick to the side of his head.

"BUCKLE!" he shouts over the sound of shattering cheekbone.

The Nazi, understandably, hits the deck but retains consciousness. Though he must think he's either dreaming or hallucinating when he looks up to see the face of Ainsley Harriott looking down at him.

"What the fuck are you doing here, Harriott, you fucking black twat?" he yells while attempting to hold his face together. Craig makes that task more difficult by running to him and again volleying him in it, knocking him clean out this time. He turns towards us.

"I'll never get tired of fucking wellying Nazis, me."

"That's highly commendable," I shout, "but we should probably get going now. I reckon our work is done, don't you?"

"Yeah, fair enough," Craig says, and begins jogging towards us. He doesn't get more than a few steps, however, before a running, out of breath policeman appears between us, his back to me and Jenny, facing Craig.

"Get in the van and start the engine," I whisper to Jenny.

"Why?"

"Coz I can't fucking drive."

"But I've only had a few lessons. And they weren't in a fucking van."

"Well you've still got more chance of operating it than I have."

She nods and creeps back towards the driver's door of the van.

The copper takes a look at the felled fascist and looks up at Craig.

"Okay, now just hold it right there, Mr Harriott."

"Fucking leave us alone, you pig. That cunt over there tried to jerk me chicken. It was self-defence."

I motion at Craig for him to simply run and get into the back of the van.

"Alright, but I still need you to stay where you are, sir." He starts talking into his radio and I see that Craig senses an ideal opportunity to act. Instead of following my instructions and simply running, though, he leans down, his head pointing forward like an untrained sprinter about to start a race.

"Ready, steady, COCK!" he yells, and charges towards the copper like an angry bull. Before he has a chance to react, the copper takes the top of Craig's head directly into his bollocks.

"AAARGH, FUCKING HELL, AINSLEY!"

He goes down and I jump into the van, shouting for Jenny to drive. She does so, but as Craig attempts to jump into the van the policeman recovers sufficiently to be able to grab his ankle and pull him back. Craig reaches out to me and I grab his hand, trying to pull him into the van. Not knowing what's going on, Jenny keeps driving, with me hanging out, forming a bizarre chain with Craig and the copper.

As Jenny drives us up the street, people stop and stare at the surreal sight. Craig desperately attempts to kick the copper loose. The copper looks up past him for the first time and locks eyes with me. The shock in his eyes when he sees a second Harriott is clear, and he appears at this point to lose all his fight. He simply lets go of Craig, rolling and tumbling in the road before finally coming to a stop in the gutter.

I finally manage to haul Craig into the back of the van. As I pull the doors closed I look up, and see the copper being helped to his feet by shocked onlookers. Craig and I collapse, exhausted.

Jenny shouts through to us.

"Can I pull this thing over?"

We get into the front and Craig takes over the driving. He takes us to a garage he'd hired where he removes the false plates before we drive back to his studio. We check social media and our attack is trending everywhere. Mobile phone footage reveals the extent of the damage the three scat-bombs did, and it's pretty glorious.

Further checks find no mention of us, or of three people or a white van, so for now, at least, I think we're in the clear.

"I think maybe we need to knock this on the head now, don't you?" I say.

Outro

THREE MONTHS LATER

A few newspaper or online articles still crop up about the *Scatbomb* campaign. One or two reports on the late night editions of the local news. At first it was every day. Then once a week. Now it's every couple of months. Give it six more months and there'll be none. Give it three years and people probably won't believe it ever happened. Sometimes even I struggle to believe it.

Despite her eagerness to be a part of it, Jenny was more than happy to let her first attack be her last one. In the absence of any such activity, I agreed to try and find a less illegal activity we could enjoy together. After a few abortive attempts at various things, from golf to kickboxing, we've settled surprisingly on badminton. For now.

Dad's rehabilitation from his stroke is going well. His speech is pretty much back to normal. He's just developed a slight Verbal Kint-esque shuffle when he walks, due to lack of movement on his left side. We're trying family therapy with a new therapist. Even Ben, freshly divorced, is joining us for some sessions. I try not to wind him up as much as I used to but it's too hard to resist at times. His divorce and the shedding of a couple of stone in weight haven't really made him any less of a cunt.

Craig has set up a consultancy firm, running some sort of educational outreach scheme for prisoners. I dread to think what he's teaching them. He still runs Buckle Productions on the side, though I think he keeps the two separate. Well, I know he does, because he persuaded me to help him run both his ventures a couple of days a week.

Unsurprisingly, my request to drop hours at CUltureSHock was greeted by Eddie with a shrug and a "Yeah, okay". I may only be here three days a week now but I make a genuine effort to do more actual work in those three days than I did before. Though I'm still not quite clear on what the company actually does. I'll never be a conscientious worker, but I'm trying not to be too much of a piss-taker.

Now, I'm sitting at my desk, scrolling through various websites, looking for the next trend of the day, when something catches my eye. It's a tweet, just four short words tweeted in response to an innocuous post by a female TV chef.

Fuck off dyke bitch, it says.

I feel an odd shudder pass through my body. I take some deep breaths, click to a file hidden within several other files on my PC, and make a note of his name and social media details. I feel my hands trembling and my heart beating faster so I open my draw and take out the Diazepam. I pop a tablet into my hand, but instead of ingesting it I just stare at it. Then I stare at it some more. I stare at it for a few long minutes before I throw it into the bin. I take the box and pop every other tablet into the bin too, before doing the same with the Amitriptyline.

I tie the bin bag and slam the drawer shut.

If you enjoyed *The Last Sane Man on Earth*, why not try our other Armley Press titles?

Available in Kindle and paperback from Amazon, and through UK bookshops.

Ray Brown: *In All Beginnings*

P. James Callaghan: *Thurso*

Mark Connors: *Stickleback*

Mark Connors: *Tom Tit and the Maniacs*

A.J. Kirby: *The Lost Boys of Prometheus City*

John Lake: *Hot Knife*

John Lake: *Blowback*

John Lake: *Speedbomb*

John Lake: *Amy and the Fox*

Mick McCann: *Coming Out as a Bowie Fan in Leeds, Yorkshire, England*

Mick McCann: *Nailed*

Mick McCann: *How Leeds Changed the World: Encyclopaedia Leeds*

Chris Nickson: *Leeds, the Biography: A History of Leeds in Short Stories*

Nathan O'Hagan: *The World is (Not) a Cold Dead Place*

Nathan O'Hagan: *Out of the City*

Samantha Priestley: *Reliability of Rope*

Samantha Priestley: *A Bad Winter*

David Siddall: *Breaking Even*

K.D. Thomas: *Fogbow and Glory*

Ivor Tymchak: *Sex and Death and Other Stories*

Michael Yates: *20 Stories High*

Visit us at armleypress.com and look for Armley Press on Facebook and Twitter.

Lightning Source UK Ltd.
Milton Keynes UK
UKHW012218090620
364731UK00004B/1298